ALSO BY BIL WRIGHT

When the Black Girl Sings
Sunday You Learn How to Box

SIMON & SCHUSTER BFYR

NEW YORK   LONDON   TORONTO   SYDNEY   NEW DELHI

Putting Makeup on the Fat Boy

Bil Wright

SIMON & SCHUSTER BFYR

An imprint of Simon & Schuster Children's Publishing Division
1230 Avenue of the Americas, New York, New York 10020

This book is a work of fiction. Any references to historical events, real people, or real locales are used fictitiously. Other names, characters, places, and incidents are products of the author's imagination, and any resemblance to actual events or locales or persons, living or dead, is entirely coincidental.

SIMON & SCHUSTER BFYR is a trademark of Simon & Schuster, Inc.
For information about special discounts for bulk purchases, please contact Simon & Schuster Special Sales at 1-866-506-1949 or business@simonandschuster.com.
The Simon & Schuster Speakers Bureau can bring authors to your live event. For more information or to book an event, contact the Simon & Schuster Speakers Bureau at 1-866-248-3049 or visit our website at www.simonspeakers.com.
Also available in a SIMON & SCHUSTER BFYR hardcover edition
Book design by Laurent Linn
The text for this book is set in Augustal.
Manufactured in the United States of America
First SIMON & SCHUSTER BFYR paperback edition August 2012
2 4 6 8 10 9 7 5 3
The Library of Congress has cataloged the hardcover edition as follows:
Wright, Bil.
Putting makeup on the fat boy / Bil Wright.
p. cm.

Summary: Sixteen-year-old Carlos Duarte is on the verge of realizing his dream of becoming a famous makeup artist, but first he must face his jealous boss at a Macy's cosmetics counter, his sister's abusive boyfriend, and his crush on a punk-rocker classmate.

ISBN 978-1-4169-3996-2 (hc)
[1. Makeup artists—Fiction. 2. Family life—New York (State)—New York—Fiction.
3. Single-parent families—Fiction. 4. Hispanic Americans—Fiction. 5. High school—Fiction. 6. Schools—Fiction. 7. Homosexuality—Fiction. 8. New York (N.Y.)—Fiction.]
1. Title.
PZ7.W9335 Pu 2011
[Fic]
2010032450
ISBN 978-1-4169-4004-3 (pbk)
ISBN 978-1-4424-2398-5 (eBook)

*This is dedicated to everyone who
wants to make the world prettier.*

ACKNOWLEDGMENTS

Thank you to my family and my loving friends.
Thank you to David and Navah and Regina.
Big hugs to Sydney and Lee-Lee.

A special thanks to Nicholas Anthony Pepe for
sharing his expertise on the cosmetics industry.

Putting Makeup on the Fat Boy

chapter 1

When I was twelve, I convinced my mother to let me do her makeup for Parents' Night. When I was finished, my sister, Rosalia, who was fifteen, said, "Ma, aren't ya even gonna say anything?"

Ma said to me, "All right, so it looks nice, Carlos. But I don't think I should be encouraging something like this. I'm not gonna go to your school and tell your teacher, 'See my face! Isn't it pretty? My son did my makeup. Didn't he do an excellent job?'"

Rosalia asked, "Why not?"

Ma said, "You know why not! Don't make me say it."

Rosalia put her hands on her hips. "You know what, Ma? Carlos is *talented*, that's what he is. He's probably gonna be famous one day for being so talented, and you should be happy he can do something this good so young!"

After Ma went to Parents' Night, Rosalia and I went to McDonald's. Rosalia told me again she thought I was talented and that I was gonna be famous. I asked her to buy me an extra bag of chocolate chip cookies and an all-chocolate sundae to prove she really meant it.

. . . .

By the time I got to Sojourner Truth/John F. Kennedy Freedom High School, I knew if other people could get paid as makeup artists, I could too. I already had a job after school being an assistant to all the teachers in a day care program. I didn't love my job, but I did love being able to go shopping for makeup at Little Ricky's on Thirteenth Street, where they had the wildest stuff. I'd run home, lock my bedroom door, and try it out immediately. Sitting on the side of my bed, studying my face in my two-sided makeup mirror (one for normal view, one for super-close-up) was like school after school. It was me practicing the thing that I knew would make me famous someday.

No matter what any of them said, the girls at school had to admit I was an expert. And the boys who got away with eyeliner because they were supposedly rockers even asked me for tips on how to put it on straight. I was really happy to tell them, because crooked eyeliner is so whack, it makes me nuts.

My friend Angie suggested, "Carlos, now that you're sixteen, you should come to Macy's and try to get a part-time job at a makeup counter." She worked there on Saturdays and she bugged me from the beginning of school in September. "You have to go and apply for a job before the holidays. That's when they need all the help they can get. I bet you could work for any company you wanted—Chanel, Bobbi Brown, Dolce & Gabbana. Any of them."

I know it sounds like I'm exaggerating, but the idea of it made me stop breathing for . . . well, a few seconds at least. I don't know why I hadn't thought of it first. I guess I'd only pictured doing Mary J. Blige's makeup before a concert, or maybe Rihanna's, or taking a month off from school to go on tour with Janet Jackson because she insisted if she didn't have me she couldn't do the tour. I hadn't thought about working at a department store.

Even though I was sure of what I could do, I thought working for Macy's was a long shot, a fantasy that was nice to talk and dream about, but soooo unlikely.

I asked her, "Angie, do you think a big, famous store like Macy's would really hire me? I don't have any professional experience."

And good old Angie said, "Honey, all we have to do is get you an application. Then we'll come up with a fake résumé. We'll put my cell number on it. When they call, I'll answer, 'Greenberg's Department Store' and tell them, 'Carlos Duarte? You'd be lucky to get him! He's fabulous!'"

Angie worked on the tenth floor in the Linens department at Macy's. But selling pillowcases and Martha Stewart sheet sets didn't mean she knew a whole lot about how they hired people in the makeup department. "I'm pretty sure it's not that easy, Angie. Can't you make friends with somebody at one of the counters and ask them how they hire?"

And of course Angie said in her typical *I-was-just-playin'-'cause-I-don't-really-have-enuff-courage-to-do-what-I-said* Angie way, "I can't go down there! They all look so beautiful . . . and so *mean*."

"Are you kidding me? 'They all look so beautiful'? I've passed by makeup counters hundreds of times, including the ones at Macy's, and the people who work at those counters have on a ton of makeup, but that doesn't mean they're beautiful! And if they look mean, maybe it's because it's hot standing around under those fluorescent lights wearing that much makeup whether you want to or not. Can you just get over yourself and go down and ask them? Get me a stupid application? This is important! And besides, it was *your* idea in the first place!"

"Maybe if I lose five pounds by Saturday when I go to work, I'll get up the courage to ask one of them."

"But, Angie, they don't care how much you weigh! And I guarantee you, you have a prettier face than most of them. Look, if you want, I'll get up early on Saturday and come over to your apartment and do your makeup. That way maybe when you see that your makeup looks better than most of theirs, you'll be able to get up enough courage to help your very best friend get the job you know he deserves!"

As usual, when Angie's insecurity took over her brain, everything I liked about her, including her common sense, suddenly disappeared. "If you want the job that badly, why don't you just show up and ask them yourself?" She was all huffed up.

"Angie, it was brilliant of you to think that I should apply there for a job. And I totally mean brilliant. But that makes sense, because *you're* brilliant. Most of the time. But now, could you tell me what sense it makes for me to go there on Saturday and *ask* how I can apply for a job and what would make me qualified, then show up there the *next* Saturday acting like I've had so much experience? I mean, what do I say when they ask me, 'If you have so much experience doing this, why did you need to come in and ask how somebody gets hired to do it in the first place?'"

Angie was losing it. "I don't know! Just tell them you thought maybe different department stores had different ways of doing things!"

"Yeah, and that would make me sound like I'd worked in dozens and dozens of them, wouldn't it?" I shook my head sadly like I couldn't believe Angie was trying to snatch away my dream for a career in makeup after putting it under my nose like a liver dog treat to a puppy. "Forget it, Ange." I put my hand up between us. "Don't give it another thought. Maybe I can Google it or something and find out that way." Then I added pitifully, "Thanks."

"Ohmygod, Carlos! All right! If you do my makeup, I'll go down to the first floor on my break and ask one of those mean, snotty-looking would-be models how to apply for a job there. Making it absolutely clear that I don't mean for myself! And I'll do it whether I've lost five pounds or not."

"Ooooh!" I squealed, and yes, I do definitely squeal, I have to admit it. And the more excited I am, the higher it is. "Do you promise?"

"Yessssss, I promise!" Angie rolled her eyes and shook her head. Then she said, "If you promise *me* something!"

"Anything, Ange, anything!" I knew she was gonna ask that, when we both worked at Macy's, I do her makeup every Saturday, and I was more than happy to say yes.

She looked at me very seriously and lifted her head like I better get ready, so I did. "You better promise that when you get hired there and everybody knows you and thinks you're talented and great . . ."

"And they will," I flicked my head to the side with one hand on my hip. "You know they will, girl."

"Yeah, well you better promise that no matter how popular you are, you won't start acting weird like you're embarrassed to be with me or something."

"Angie," I said, just as serious as she was, "I'm sorry you have this condition that makes you say and even think insane things. So, what I'm going to do until you can get yourself healed is just say, Hon, I love you and I'll always love you, whether you're a hundred and three pounds or three hundred and one pounds. I'm just hoping that you won't wind up being three hundred and one pounds. Because, first, it isn't healthy, and, second, you'll want to be on one of those weight-loss shows, and then I will have to disown you because I think they're just so tacky! I'd die, Ange, I really would!"

Angie said, "And I don't think we have to worry about me ever being a hundred and three pounds, unless somebody sews my mouth shut!" She laughed, one of her big old Angie laughs, which is one of my favorite sights and sounds in the world.

And I started picturing myself behind the biggest, most fabulous makeup counter in Macy's.

chapter 2

I went to Burrito Take-Out Village to brag to my sister, Rosalia, that I was going to be working at Macy's very soon, and I'd share my discount with her. I couldn't believe she was going to school to be a medical technician at a place she'd learned about from a poster on the subway. She was calling it college and working at Burrito Take-Out Village to pay for it. Okay, so getting such crummy grades that she couldn't go to a real college was no one's fault but her own. It was just that all we'd ever talked about, sitting on the side of her bed while she let me try out different combinations of eye shadow on her, was how we were not gonna end up like our mother, managing a dry cleaner's and not being able to afford anything unless it was on sale.

"I saw the cutest jacket," Ma would say. "I'm gonna keep checking back. Eventually they'll put it on sale." Or the worst was, "My boss says if somebody doesn't claim this coat in the next few weeks, he's gonna let me have it. Isn't that great!" Ugh. And we'd have to say, yeah, it was great, because neither one of us could afford to buy her a winter coat, so better an unclaimed one from the cleaner's she worked in than no decent winter coat at all. I remember having this dream once that a lady stopped us on the street and asked Ma for all the clothes she had on because the lady said they were hers. And when Ma denied it, all the cleaning tickets started to appear on her clothes, and they had the lady's name on them in huge print.

Rosalia said she used to think maybe our father would show up out of nowhere and we'd live happily ever after, but then she realized she'd been watching too many soap operas. She said she kind of remembered him from when she was little, but the only details were that he was "tall and had red eyes."

"Tall with red eyes, Rosalia? That sounds like the devil."

Rosalia laughed. "Yeah, that's pretty much how Ma describes him too." According to Ma, he left when Rosalia was five and I was two. There's one really bad picture of him that Rosalia and I saw in Ma's drawer once. It was taken outside in the dark and you could barely see what he looked like. I wouldn't know the man if I walked into the cleaner's and Ma was cursing at him, which is about what would happen. When we do bring him up, which is hardly at all these days, Ma makes this face as though she smells dog crap somewhere in the room. "If we have to talk about the drunken drug addict, I'm leaving the room," she says. And Rosalia and I look at each other and laugh. It's like a joke now, our father the joke, the smell in the room. Was he really a drunken drug addict? When I asked Ma, she said, "What? You think I'm such a crappy mother, I'd tell my kids their father was a drunken drug addict if it wasn't true?"

Ma hates all the boys she's ever seen Rosalia with, and says, "If you think you're gonna bring another bum in here for me to cook for, you're nuts." Now Rosalia's going out with this cook at Burrito Take-Out Village named Danny, so she came home and said to Ma, "This one's not a bum, Ma. And he can cook dinner for *you*. So don't start in on him."

I can't believe my sister really wants to spend the rest of her life looking at other people's X-rays. And now she's talking about getting engaged to Danny, who I have not-so-great feelings about. Maybe it's because he's never once looked me right in the eye, and because every time I go into Burrito Take-Out Village, all the other guys in the kitchen say stuff in Spanish that I don't understand, and then they laugh, and Danny doesn't exactly laugh, but he *does* snicker. If Rosalia understands, she pretends she doesn't, except once she whipped her head around and said, "Screw you. You think I'm deaf?" And the guys stopped, but they still had these smirks on their faces, including Danny. And because he's a part of all that, I'm hoping there's no chance he'll ever be my brother-in-law.

But the news about Macy's was too good to wait, even though it hadn't happened yet. So I decided to go first to Rosalia at Burrito Take-Out Village and tell her and then decide how much to tell my ma, since I knew she wouldn't be all that crazy about the makeup part.

When I got to Rosalia's job, she was busy taking orders, so I had to wait. One of the boys in the kitchen saw me come in and went farther back to where I couldn't see him and whistled and said something stupid in Spanish. Danny had already looked up from the grill when he saw me come in. As usual, he didn't say hi or anything. He just kept cooking. But when his buddy whistled and said whatever trash he did, Danny grinned. Rosalia must have been too busy to hear, or else she was ignoring it. When she finally had a second, I went up to the counter and blurted as quickly as I could, "Guess what! Angie's gonna find out how I can get a job at Macy's doing makeup on the weekends, and after they hire me, I promise to let you use my discount. Won't it be *beyond crazy fabulous!*"

I could see out of the corner of my eye Danny at the grill behind Rosalia looking at me. And next to him were two of the other guys in their dirty white uniforms staring at me like my head was spinning around while I was talking. All right, I'm not stupid. It was raining hard and I had on my black vinyl slicker and the hat that goes with it. And my mascara may even have been smudged a little from so much rain. So, I didn't look like any of the yuppies in the stupid place. Or those boys in their dirty uniforms. But I never look like anyone else, and that's the point. I don't *want* to look like anyone else. So I thought what I always think. That Danny Fernandez and his obnoxious buddies could all kiss my butt.

Rosalia didn't have time to say a whole lot. She told me in this low voice, "Carlos, your eyes are all smeary. We can talk when I get home." So I left. On the way home I decided not to tell my mother at all until I was hired.

chapter 3

The next Saturday, I got up early and went from East Fifth Street, where we lived, up to Sixteenth, where Angie lived. Her mother stared at me all over and said, "I've heard a lot about you. As close as Angie says you two are, I'm surprised I haven't met you before."

I said, "Well . . . I'm here now," and tried to make it sound intelligent even though I felt stupid as soon as I'd said it. I hadn't met her because Angie had admitted that her mother would think I was weird. So why would I volunteer to go to her house to have one more person think I was weird?

"She's back there." Angie's mother pointed, still doing her survey of me.

As I passed her parents' bedroom on the way to Angie's bedroom, her father came out in an ugly green uniform and called out, "Why's he going into Angie's room?"

Angie's mother said loudly from the kitchen, "I told you before, he's going to do her makeup." And her father said, "I still don't know what the hell that means! But whatever it means, he can do it out here!"

I was caught in the hallway, facing his big belly. I turned

right around, heading for the living room, wishing Angie would come out of her stupid bedroom already. I sat on the couch with my Vuitton Neverfull bag on my lap, trying to pretend I didn't know he was still there, observing me like I was an exotic insect. (And no, I don't have a real Vuitton, but it's the best imitation I've ever seen).

Finally, when Angie's father did go into the kitchen, there was all this whispering. It wasn't hard to figure out that he thought the circus had come to town, and Angie's mother was saying it was fine, it would be gone soon.

As soon as Angie came out, I knew we were in trouble. "If I do your makeup," I said as quietly as I could, "you can't wear that."

"What do you mean, I can't wear this!" she started whining immediately. "I love polka dots! Polka dots are my favorite. That's why I'm wearing them today. To give me courage."

"First of all, polka dots are your favorite because you're a psycho. And I don't really care if you wear them any other day but today. Today I'm doing a smoky eye for daytime in shades of gray and you should wear something subtle, like—"

"I know. You want me to wear black like those vampires at the makeup counters. And that's what you get to do after they hire you. But I don't wanna wear all black. It makes me depressed. And I have to work eight hours, telling people the difference between a king-size bed and a twin—believe it or not—so I can't afford to be depressed. I want my polka dots!"

"Then, fine!" I knew there wasn't time to try to convince her, and I certainly didn't want her parents to come rushing in from the other room to defend her. I knew her father would be only too happy to throw me out. I reached into my bag and pulled out my makeup case. "I'll work *around* the polka dots!"

About thirty minutes later, in spite of the polka dots, Angie had a daytime look to rock all of Macy's and to definitely impress the makeup counter divas. Even she was impressed, and I'd done her makeup dozens of times. "Should I tell them you did it?" she asked me.

"That's the point, Angie girl, that's the point! That, and an application!"

She called me on her morning break to say that she was too nervous to go downstairs to the makeup counters, and I tried really hard not to say anything mean enough to hurt our friendship. But I was furious. If she was that nervous, who knew if she'd ever have the guts to go down and ask *anything?* What Angie did when she was nervous was two things: She stuffed everything into her mouth that would fit, and she sweated, no matter how cold or hot it was. And she wasn't exactly a careful eater, so I could picture what her makeup would look like when she finished eating and sweating, cause I'd seen it before—lots of times.

"Angie, I won't hate you if you don't go talk to those people. I'll just be very disappointed. To be honest, I just wish I hadn't wasted my whole night worrying about the perfect look to give you, and then gotten up early this morning and worked harder than I ever worked before, just so you would feel comfortable enough to do me this one favor. And now who knows whether or not you're even gonna do it!"

There was silence on the other end. It wasn't as though she couldn't figure out I was trying to guilt-trip her. I was so desperate, I had to resort to something that pitiful in hopes she'd get a grip and do what we'd planned. But all she said was, "I'm really sorry, honey," in this frail voice like she had a temperature of 110, and pneumonia.

But at twelve thirty Miss Beyoncé Knowles's "Irreplaceable" started ringing in my jeans and I hoped for a miracle.

"Hi, Miss Angie Girl," I said gently. What I heard on the other end was a shriek.

"I did it, I did it, I did it!"

I looked up at the ceiling and said, "Thank you, God!"

"The thing is," Angie said, somehow already back to her familiar whine, "it's not as easy as we thought, Carlos! It's really hard!"

"What's really hard?" I wanted her to be clear and specific and encouraging.

She repeated, "It's a lot, Carlos! Really a lot! It's not as easy as we thought at all!"

I refused to get psyched-out without knowing the details. What was a lot for Angie didn't have to be the same from my point of view. "I didn't think it would be easy, Angie. I didn't think it would be anything, because I didn't have any information! So, what is the information you have that makes you think it will be so hard?"

"I can't tell you now. It would take too long. I'll tell you when I get home."

There were no words for how frustrated she made me. Angie is the kind of person who can tell you the weather is supposed to be sunny for the next three days and make it sound like tragic news.

"Angie, please! I've waited all morning for this. Can't you tell me *anything*?"

"No, Carlos, no! My lunchtime is almost over and I haven't had anything to eat." Well, I didn't know how that could be true, since she'd been talking with her mouth full both times she'd been on the phone. But I knew if it was a choice between me and food, I didn't have a prayer. The thing is, though, I can be just as persistent as Angie can be annoying. "All right." I gave her a big sigh, "I'll wait. But can you at least tell me what counter you went to, to ask."

Angie started giggling. I knew it had to be something incredible. "Well? You can't do this, Miss Angie! Spill it!"

"FEEEAATTTUURRE FAACCCEE!" she screamed into the phone.

I smiled. *Well! You go, Angie! If we're gonna shoot for it, let's shoot for the top!* "Angie, you know how much I love you, don't you? Even though sometimes I think somebody is paying you to make me legally insane, I do love you. And I will wait until you get home tonight to tell me what the people at the FeatureFace counter said about how fast I'll become famous working for them."

"Oooo, Carlos, I'm just warning you. It will not be easy!"

I had enough positive information now that I didn't have to even consider anything else. "Do I need an application, Angie?"

"Yes."

"And do you have one for me?"

"Yes. I had to be superpersistent, because nobody at that counter was paying any attention to anyone except—are you ready for this? Shirlena Day! "

"Shirlena Day! Was she there?"

"Yep, and everyone was running in circles trying to get all the stuff she was asking for. It was crazy, crazy! But I did manage to get you an application."

"Darling, that's all Carlos has to know."

When I shut my phone, I was already trying to figure out once I was working weekends, how long would it take before FeatureFace begged me to quit school to work for them full-time? Then I thought about Shirlena Day being a customer. I'd watched her on *Smokin' Friday Nights* a few times and I thought she was a comedic genius—especially her Michelle O. As a matter of fact, I thought she was the funniest person on the show. Why wasn't I working for FeatureFace right now? By next month I'd be right in the middle of a *Vogue* spread with Shirlena Day quoted as saying, "I discovered Carlos Duarte working behind the FeatureFace counter at Macy's, and I haven't been able to live without him since!"

I could make it happen. I knew I could. But first . . . FeatureFace had to hire me!

Chapter 4

We met at the Dunkin' Donuts halfway between Angie's house and mine. I insisted we sit at a back booth so Angie wouldn't get distracted, which she did quite easily. Especially if it was a boy with dark hair, who looked like he'd lifted any kind of weights at all. All Angie had to see was some evidence of pecs and the dark hair and it was over! She'd order another hot chocolate, two more chocolate-covered donuts, and stare. You could get up, go shopping, get your hair cut, and come back, and if the guy was still there, Angie would not have noticed you weren't. Luckily, when Angie met me to discuss Macy's and FeatureFace, there were only screaming kids and their mothers in there.

Angie hugged me like she was squeezing the last bit of Crest from the tube. "I'm so excited, Carlos! They thought my makeup was fabulous, and they can't wait for you to come in."

"Is that true?" By the time I saw Angie, her makeup was a total mess and I would have told anybody who asked that I'd had nothing to do with it.

She reached into her bag and pulled out the application. Unfortunately, it had some grease stains and tiny bits of cheese on it, which didn't please me, but that was Angie. Anything that Angie touched eventually got touched by food.

Before I could even look at the application, her face changed completely. It was the now-I-have-something-too-tragic-to-tell-you face. "The thing is, Carlos, while I was there, there was this other poor girl there who was being interviewed. They were barely paying her any attention because Shirlena Day was there. But I saw how they do it." Angie shook her head like we were suddenly in a funeral home staring down at a coffin, with my chances of ever working for FeatureFace in it.

"This girl had her résumé there, and the counter manager was going over it, kind of—like I said, he was too busy making sure Shirlena Day got whatever she wanted. But then he'd come back and look at the girl's résumé and say mean things about it."

"Whadya mean, 'mean things'?"

"Oh, you know, like 'I've never heard of this place' or 'They didn't keep you there very long, did they?' It was awful. I felt so sorry for the girl. Then he'd get distracted because a salesperson would ask for something that Shirlena Day wanted, and he'd snap at them like they were idiots because he wanted them to say yes to her, even if it seemed like they were out of something."

"Was Shirlena nice or was she a creep?" I asked Angie. Who knew? She might be a complete terror in a department store, dealing with the *little* people.

"No," Angie said, "she seemed pretty nice. She kept telling them, 'I can have my assistant phone in an order,' but they wanted to seal the deal on the spot. So every time she mentioned something she liked that FeatureFace made, they went crazy, bringing out cases and cases of it."

"I can't stand it, Ange," I squealed. "I wish I'd been there. I wish I could've been working for them already. She would've loved me and I would've loved her, and that would have been it!"

"I'm tellin ya'," Angie said, slurping hot chocolate, "ya gotta get the job first, ya gotta get past this dude Valentino. And he's like a guard dog." Her mouth was so covered with sugar, she looked like she was wearing frosted lip- stick. "Because the counter was so hysterical, I had to wait forever before I could even speak to him. After he finished insulting the girl's résumé, he said, 'I don't suppose you have a portfolio, do you?' And I thought, She's toast now, burnt freakin' toast! But she had this book of pictures of the makeup she'd done. I didn't see the pictures, but all I kept thinking was you probably don't have any pictures like that, do you?"

"No . . . ," I said, annoyed both that Angie was so sure of what I didn't have and also that she was right.

"Then, she had this model with her. So after this Valentino guy looked at her book, he told her to go ahead and make up her model, which is when I got a chance to talk to him." By now, of course, instead of sounding like *any* of it was good news, Angie sounded like it had all been a disaster. She used it as an excuse to get up to order two more donuts. But while she was waiting for them, I was fig- uring out how to get what I needed to at least have a shot at getting what I wanted.

Before she even sat down again, I called out to her, "So you said this guy really liked your makeup?"

"Yeah," Angie answered, waiting for her donuts. She didn't even ask me if I wanted anything.

"Was he nice to you?"

"No!" she said, coming back to our booth. She practically swallowed a whole donut in one bite. "He answered my questions like I was a piece of lint on his shoulder and he couldn't understand why I wouldn't fall off."

"But you say he liked your makeup," I insisted.

"Yeah. He liked it a lot. I mean, he didn't go on and on or anything. He just said, 'Your makeup is very well done' in this voice like even if I was a piece of lint, at least I was lint with a good makeup job."

"Then I'm gonna take your picture in the exact same makeup, and another one with a different outfit. And I'll get Rosalia to do the same thing. And Soraya, and Chantal at school. Maybe I won't have a lot of pictures, but the ones I have will be *beyond stunning!*"

Everybody deserves a chance, especially those who are as talented as I am, I thought. I made Angie sit right there at Dunkin' Donuts and help me fill out the application. I knew I could get at least two of the guys who owned beauty salons in our neighborhood to say I'd worked as a makeup artist for them. Plus we added a couple of salons at the bottom of the list that we knew had gone out of business, so they couldn't be traced. The good part, I figured, was that I was young. How many places could I have worked?

The next week at school I did makeup on Chantal and Soraya and took pictures. I did a step-by-step with Chantal, which I thought was a genius idea, because it would show I really knew what I was doing and how I could change somebody's look completely. Chantal really got on my nerves during the photos and started asking how much she was getting paid, so I finally had to give her twenty-five dollars. But it taught me that when you ask somebody to do you a favor as your friend: (1) make sure they know what the word "favor" means, and (2) make sure they really are your friend. The reason I was hoping all the girls would not expect to get paid was because I was already paying this kid at school, Gleason Kraft, sixty dollars to take the pictures. So practically my whole paycheck from the day care center was used up. It really pissed me off that Chantal said she'd do it as my friend and then asked for money. If she didn't look exactly like Alek Wek, the supermodel, I would have told her to forget it and that she was lucky I'd ever considered using her at all.

Gleason Kraft was a rocker who was also in the photography club, and I knew he'd be great because I'd seen his photographs of concerts displayed around school. They looked like they were right out of magazines. He was in my homeroom, but the way I got to be friends with him was by telling him about products I knew he'd like for his rocker look. I told him that I knew a lot of rockers bought their makeup at Ricky's and there was one right near school. I also told him his hair was incredible when he dyed it jet black. He had this thick biracial hair thing going—you know, part curly, part fuzzy—and the way it looked with his gray eyes was insane! He looked a little embarrassed when I was going on and on like a twelve-year-old girl about his hair, but he also looked like he didn't mind the attention. If the world was perfect, I'd probably date Gleason Kraft, but only my dreams are perfect. Before I started flirting with him and giving him hair and makeup tips, I don't think Gleason Kraft knew that Carlos Duarte even existed.

I told my girl Soraya, "I'm going to get a job at Macy's working for FeatureFace, and I have to do your makeup and take pictures of it."

Soraya is a manager at Tokyo Jo's on Eleventh St. It's a resale store where they sell top designer's clothes for a whole lot less. I don't get why exactly. As far as I can tell, there's not anything wrong with them. Even at the resale price, I can't usually afford them. When I told her I was getting the job, Soraya, who thinks managing Tokyo Jo's has made her Anna Wintour of *Vogue*, tried to correct me in her fake British accent. "You mean you have an interview, deah."

The truth was, I'd called the FeatureFace counter myself and spoken to this girl who sounded superflaky, but she'd said yes, they were hiring, and someone would get back to me.

"No, I'm going to work for them, Soraya, just like I said. I just haven't told them yet."

That's when I think my girl got that we were making history. "Then you should do my pictures in the store," she said. "Give them makeup *and* haute couture!" Soraya put on a vintage Yves Saint Laurent, and we took mad pictures.

For Angie's shoot we went into a Catholic church that has prayer hours every day from twelve to one, so we went when we were on lunch. Angie thought it was weird, but that's because Angie doesn't have any sense of what a beauty shoot is. I've had subscriptions to *Vogue* and *Harper's Bazaar* since I was fourteen and could save up for them, so I knew that what I was doing was *beyond genius*. Gleason was going nuts shooting Angie in front of all the votive candles. For him it was photographer's heaven!

Finally it was time for Rosalia's pictures. I decided to take them in front of a bodega right across the street from Quik Clean & Press, the cleaner's my Ma managed. I wanted her to be proud of me, and one way of doing it was to let her look right across the street and see me telling a photographer how I wanted a picture of a model to look, and to have that model be her daughter. Also, no matter what she thought about me doing makeup, she had to get that it was an honest-to-God professional job and that I was serious.

That Friday I still hadn't heard whether FeatureFace even wanted to see me. But I knew I was going ahead with the shoot anyway. I'd convinced Rosalia not to say anything to Ma, so it would be a surprise.

Rosalia's version of family support that day was "You better make this good! And remember I gotta get to work, so don't take a lotta time!" I love my sister, but she has no idea about art or creativity. The point was, it was something Ma could be proud of, and Rosalia would be a part of it, whether she got it or not.

Now, it's not as though Rosalia owns anything that isn't too tight everywhere, like every other girl in our neighborhood and school. She loves to show her boobs and her butt, no matter how big they look coming at you or walking away from you, but it just wasn't the look I was going for. So I told Gleason to focus on her face, her makeup. Rosalia thought she was doing the cover of *Cosmo*, and she was dressed like the Hooker from Hoochieville. Not the look I wanted.

We went across the street to the bodega, and I knew Ma

was in Quik Clean & Press, but I pretended I didn't even know the place existed. Angie was there as my assistant, and Gleason was in his pointy-toed boots and blue leather jacket, and people were stopping to watch us. I made Rosalia look pretty fierce, and even got her to let me put her hair back, which she hated, being the queen of superbig hair. I don't mean cool big like Gleason's. I mean, like, clown big. But I kept telling her, "Please, Rosalia, it's about the makeup. They can't see your makeup if they have to look through a hedge!" And she didn't love it, but she agreed to let me calm her hair down, way down.

We hadn't been there five minutes before my mother came out of the cleaner's. "Carlos! What are you doing?" she yelled across the street.

"It's a photo shoot, Ma! It's for FeatureFace Cosmetics! For Macy's!"

She stood there for a minute, with the cars going between us, her arms folded. Rosalia, of course, waved and yelled out, "Hi, Ma! I hate my hair!" So we lost a little of the professional atmosphere I was going for. But I could see that Ma was impressed. I've seen actual shoots for magazines, with trailers and those big reflectors and stuff, and we didn't look anything like that, but it still looked like Ma thought we were doing something important, so I was glad. Of course, if the president of either FeatureFace or Macy's happened to be anywhere near, they'd probably sue me for using their name in a big lie, but if they were there, I haven't heard about it yet.

I could feel when Ma wasn't there anymore, but I knew there'd be questions when I got home.

•   •   •

"No, I haven't gotten the call yet, but I know it's coming and I have to be ready."

"Well, you're just a kid and they never heard of you, so don't get your hopes up," Ma told me at dinner. It was just her and me, since Rosalia was already at work.

A few mouthfuls later Ma asked me, "Do they even hire boys to do that at Macy's?" as though it was something really obscene I was hoping to do.

"Ma," I said as patiently as I could, "you've been to Macy's. The whole first floor is full of men who are makeup artists."

"I never noticed," Ma said. She shrugged. "Well, like I said, you're a kid with no experience, so don't count on anything."

By the next Tuesday there was still no call from FeatureFace. I decided it meant God was giving me more time to get my act together. I thought about getting a book out of the library about how to interview for a job—a life-changing job, not being an assistant at a day care center, taking three-year-olds to the bathroom and getting projectile-vomited on at least once a week. I thought, *If I want to convince these people I'm going to be a star, I should interview like one.* So I watched talk shows like *Inside the Actors Studio*, where actors talked about how they got famous. I sat on my bed and leaned back to look relaxed, and smiled and talked out loud about how I knew that I was born to make people beautiful and how it was my personal campaign to stop people from acting ugly and they'd see how much better they looked.

When I did practice in the mirror, I was proud of myself. From the time I'd left junior high school, I'd looked like a different person. I'd dried out my zits (I used to call my own face the Field of Zits) with Teen Skin Alarm, and the only oil I went near was Olay. I'd given up potato chips, onion rings, french fries, fried rice, and donuts. Which also meant, at least in my mind, that I wasn't fat anymore, I was *big*. And *big* could mean anything—unlike "fat," which only meant one thing: FAT.

I decided to always walk into a room like I was deciding if I *wanted* to stay, not if I'd be *allowed* to. Angie used to say she thought I should go into theater or the movies. When I asked her if it was because she thought I was such a good actor or singer, she said, "No. It's because I honestly think the red carpet was invented for you!"

Even though by Wednesday morning there was still no call, I decided I only had two days to get my outfit together if I was going for my interview on Saturday. I went to Tokyo Jo's after school to see Soraya. Every once in a while she has something so marked down, she saves it for me, and sometimes it's so ugly that it's obvious why nobody else bought it. But sometimes it's truly a score nine and a half or a ten, and I can't resist it. I didn't really think I'd find anything for my interview that was in my budget, but I couldn't *not* look either. I wanted to show up at Macy's looking like I didn't need the job, but like they'd be lucky to get me.

"I think it's crazy to spend money when they haven't even called you yet," Soraya said before I could even close the store door behind me.

I tried on a pair of Cavalli pants that were too long and a little too tight, not to mention too expensive.

"You're such a shortie," she teased me. "You should go to a designer store for little kids."

"I would," I told her, "except I still wouldn't be able to afford anything."

My last try was an olive green turtleneck sweater by a company called Turtle that I'd never heard of. But that's exactly what I looked like in it, a turtle with hair, wearing a sweater. I should have known better. Maybe it's true that people with tan skin look good in olive green, but like with a lot of other things, I guess I'm the exception.

I'd given up, although I never really give up, so I told Soraya, "You have to keep your eye out for something, Soraya. A sweater, a shirt, a vest. I can't go get hired looking ordinary. I have to go there *owning* my new job!"

"You should go to the Gap," Soraya teased me. "You're a high school kid with a babysitting job at a day care center, and you wanna be *all that!*"

"I *am* all that!" I laughed. "Always have been, always will be. And don't you forget it!"

I was almost out of the store when I saw them, hanging from the ceiling in the corner, like someone was coming through from the roof feetfirst. All you could see were these thigh-high Stella McCartney boots. They were *beyond excellent.*

"Ohmygod! Soraya! They're beautiful!"

"I know," Soraya said like a cat that'd just had three cans of Friskies, as though she owned the Stella McCartneys herself.

"I want to try them on!"

"They're girls' boots, Carlos!"

"Duh! I still want to try them on!"

"They're also three hundred dollars, marked down from six hundred. They're not for playing dress-up with!"

"Soraya, there is nobody in here. It's not as though you're busy. Can you please get the boots down so I can try them on!"

"You are such a pain, Carlos! I don't know why I even put up with you!"

I just smiled at her, patiently, while she went to the back to get a ladder.

Sitting on Soraya's little stool behind the counter, I pulled on the six-hundred-reduced-to-three-hundred-dollar boots. I didn't hate for a second that they had at least five-inch heels. "Fierce!" I gasped. I stood and headed for the mirror.

"If my boss came in right now, I could kiss this job toodles!" Soraya moaned.

"You're lying, and you know it. You boss doesn't care who or what tries this stuff on as long as they have the credit card to make it happen."

"And you don't, so could you please be careful in them!"

"Mami," I told her, "they are indestructible! Trust me!" And then, as I turned back and forth in the mirror, getting the front and the back view, it hit me. I took a moment. I wanted to be sure it came out exactly right.

"Soraya, honey," I started.

"You don't even have half the money, so don't even think about it. And besides, I told you, they're girls'!" Soraya snapped.

"How could you work in this place and be so backward, Soraya? I mean, really! I'm embarrassed for you! Who is separating men's from women's clothes anymore? It's not like I tried on a bra! They're boots, for crapsake! Black, fabulous boots that fit me and make my legs look incredible and make me look like a star, and that's all that matters. That's what all clothes are supposed to do. They don't define whether you can give birth or not! Now, if you are really my friend and have any fashion sense at all, you will admit how *beyond excellent* these look on me, and you will do me a huge, huge favor!"

"No!" Soraya said as soon as I'd gotten the *r* in "favor" out of my mouth.

"But you don't even know what I'm asking."

"If it has anything to do with those boots leaving the store without you giving me three hundred dollars, the answer is no. No!"

I didn't once take my eyes off myself in the boots. I stood firmly in them as though they'd been designed for me and I was reunited with them at last.

"Soraya, what I want you to do is to be calm and listen to me. This is me, Carlos. Your friend. I am dependable. Trustworthy. Smart. And I'm going to be rich enough one day to buy four pairs of these in one shopping trip without even thinking twice about it. So I want you to really pay attention to who is asking you what I'm about to ask you."

"Darling, I know who is about to ask me something. You are Carlos Duarte, and you're a crazy person. And I don't even want to hear it."

I had no choice but to get it out fast. "Soraya, I want you to let me wear these just for the interview, which means a couple of hours. Not a day, not a half day. A couple of *hours*. I will wear some other shoes to the store, change into the Stellas in the men's room, and only wear them for my interview. When the interview is over, I will go back to the men's room—"

"In my store's ladies' boots!"

"And change into my own shoes. I may be crazy, but I'm honest, and you know it. Please. I would *so* do it for you. I promise on my life—no, on my *career*—that I won't let anything happen to them. Please. I will never ask you for anything ever again. Please." I stopped and posed in the boots. A subtle pose, but so she could tell how intensely fabulous they looked on me.

"I caaaannnn't, Carlos. I caaaannn't."

I sat down again and took the boots off as quickly as I could. Standing in my socks, holding them against my chest, I pleaded in almost a whisper. "I swear I'll come in the same day, just before I have to go for my interview, and come back right afterward." I took a step closer and leaned toward her, looking like a shoeless beggar in another country. "I know these will help me get the job, Soraya. I know it. I knew it as soon as I saw them. Of course, if I had the money like some of the rich kids who come in here and just throw down their credit cards, I would do it. But I can't. Do you think I want to be here begging like this, to *borrow* shoes?" Then I had an idea. "Do you want me to give you money? I could!" Soraya looked horrified. "I could give you maybe a hundred dollars if I save it from my pay, and then when I bring them back and they're exactly the same as when I left, you could give me my hundred dollars back!"

"Carlos! That is so gross! I can't believe you thought of that!" Soraya scrunched up her face and looked pretty unattractive doing it. "No, I wouldn't take your money. I wouldn't. I'm just so afraid . . ."

But I knew she was closer than she had been at the beginning.

"I know you're afraid. Because you're a responsible person. And that's why you're a good manager. And I respect that. That's why I wouldn't do anything to screw that up. I swear." I made my voice even lower and more vulnerable-sounding. "Soraya, if I let anything happen to these boots, you have every right to never speak to me again. Plus, you'll have my hundred dollars."

"I told you already, Carlos, I wouldn't take your money. No offense. I just mean, how could I? We're supposed to be friends." She sighed this incredibly deep sigh. "I have to think about it. I have to."

I knew to keep my mouth shut. I quietly put my sneakers back on and wiped the toes of the boots with my hands, gently, signaling to Soraya how valuable I knew the Stella McCartneys were. I eased my sunglasses down from the top of my head to the tip of my nose. I looked over them at her doe-eyed, like Bambi. "I guess I'll go. You let me know . . . what you decide." I turned and started slowly toward the door.

Before I could open it, she blurted out, "Oh, you're such a little actor, Carlos! How am I supposed to say no to you!"

I swung around not quite believing it was happening.

"But you know you could get me fired, don't you? And I need this job!"

"I won't do one single thing to jeopardize your job, Soraya Sweetmeats, not one single thing!"

"And you have to keep your word. You pick them up the day of, and you don't put them on until before the interview, and you take them off immediately after, and you bring them the bloody hell here as soon as you can!"

I loved her when she tried to use her fake British accent. It was so fake and so awful, but I'd seen her use it on customers, and they fell for it.

"I bloody will!" I said, sounding like Queen Elizabeth herself. I hugged the boots, and she grabbed them from me. "Don't touch these until you come back for your appointment. And don't be looking around the shop for anything else to try to scam me out of!"

"I adore you, Soraya. I truly do adore you and your fake British ass!"

I left Tokyo Jo's thinking it almost didn't matter what else I walked up to the FeatureFace counter wearing. I'd have on thigh-high Stella McCartney boots, looking like I'd designed the makeup for anybody I said I had. FeatureFace better be ready. Carrlos Duarte was coming. They just better be ready. That was if, of course, they ever called me.

Chapter 5

Friday morning it happened. I was in history class when my thigh vibrated.

I got up and ran out, even though it's totally against the rules. "Hello, hello!" I shouted in the hallway.

"This is Valentino, the manager of FeatureFace Cosmetics at Macy's." He said it like he was saying, *This is Meryl Streep, and I've been nominated for a zillion Oscars.* "Is Carlos Duarte there?"

"This is Carlos," I said, trying to sound like Meryl too, except in *The Devil Wears Prada.*

"We want to see you tomorrow for an interview. We have two slots available. An eleven and a one thirty."

As soon as he got out "One thirty," I said, "Eleven."

"Fine. Bring your résumé and a model for your makeup demonstration."

"Of course," I said, like it was old, old information for a pro like me.

"Don't be late. We have a very full schedule on Saturday and we don't tolerate lateness." Now *he* was definitely Meryl in *Prada.*

"I won't. I'm never late," I babbled. "Thank you." But he didn't hear any of it, because he'd already hung up.

I started the conversation with myself right then and there. Everyone has these conversations, I know, and usually people say conversations with yourself are in people's minds, but that's not true with me. Because it always feels like the conversation is traveling through my whole body. If it's going one way, it stays in my head for a while before it moves on. Sometimes it goes to my throat really quickly and my throat gets tight, or into my heart, or my heart and my throat at the same time, but all the parts answer one way or another. And this conversation about the model for my test, who it should be and what I should do with her, filled my head and my stomach and my heart, hands, legs, ankles, and feet.

As soon as I got out of school, I started toward Burrito Take-Out Village. I wasn't sure all the time what Rosalia's schedule was, but I knew if she wasn't there, she'd be there soon. I'd wait outside. But, as it turned out, I didn't have to. God knew I had important business to take care of.

"So you want one quesadilla with cheese, and one cheese and chicken burrito combo—with black beans and two Diet Cokes. Sorry, I mean Pepsis. And it's to go."

My sister looked at me standing inside the door, but didn't say anything.

"It'll be a few minutes. You want chips with that?" she asked the couple standing in front of her.

The guy said "Yes," and the girl said "No" at the same time. They laughed. Then the guy said, "It's up to you.

You're the one who said you're on a diet."

"If I was really on my diet, I'd be having a salad," the girl said.

So the guy told my sister, "Yeah, chips."

I waited for Rosalia to give me a sign that she could speak to me. She turned toward the kitchen and yelled out, "Quesadilla with cheese. Cheese chicken burrito—with black beans," with a Spanish accent I only heard when she was working there.

Then she said, "Come over here!" to me like she'd already told me and I hadn't obeyed her. I was just trying to respect her job and not interrupt. Of course, when she said it, Danny looked up from the grill. He turned his head away from both of us to the kitchen and said something softly. Two of the other worker bees poked their heads out of the kitchen toward the counter. They disappeared, but I heard, in a loud squeaky voice, *"Mariquita, maricón!"* and then these squeals. At first Rosalia was trying to pretend she wasn't hearing any of it.

"What's up?" she asked me. The squeals got louder.

I said, "I wanted to tell you something, but I think maybe it's not a good time."

She looked at me, and I could see she was frustrated. "I'm sorry, Carlos. They're idiots. What can I say?"

"Mariquita, mariquita!"

I made a face in their direction even though I couldn't see any of them.

"I'll see you at home, Rosalia."

Immediately I heard from the kitchen, "See-you-at-home-Rosalia-mariquita!"

Rosalia turned and kind of yelled-whined back, "Yoouu guuuys!" But I was on my way out of there.

"Screw all of you!" I said as soon as I got out. "Such tough little he-men! Yeah, *right!*"

chapter 6

Okay, historic day requires historic look, yes? It only makes sense. So, black almost-skinny jeans, which Angie says make me look like I have mosquito legs, only from the knees down. Like she knows what mosquito legs look like. Black pin-striped men's suit jacket cut like it's from the thirties. I got it from Soraya a year ago at a steal because it was hanging in Tokyo Jo's window too long and got a little faded. So I dyed it. It lost the pinstripes, unfortunately, but I still love the way it fits. Double-breasted on a chunker can sometimes be a really sad look, but on me this thing is L'uomo Vogue!

I also had on my red sneakers, which would come off as soon as I got to Macy's, just like I'd promised Soraya-Anna-Wintour. Under my arm, a red vinyl combination book bag and binder. I used it to carry my fake résumé and the pictures Gleason had taken of my own version of *America's Next Top Model*—from the neck up anyway. The vinyl bag was actually for a kid, and I found it in a Duane Reade back-to-school-supplies aisle. But I swear I could have passed it off as a Gucci original.

Three fingertips full of gel in my hair so it looked shower fresh, but not like I'd put Wesson cooking oil in it, a look I detest. My eyes were clear. I had just the slightest touch of color in my cheeks. I'd given myself a manicure. I looked *beyond excellent!*

And everybody knew it when I stomped into Macy's like Tyra Banks stomping down the Victoria's Secret runway that one last time. Except I was ARRIVING!

I was arriving without my model. When I finally got to tell Rosalia I'd picked her to come with me to Macy's and be my model, she acted as though I'd asked her to loan me money. "All right," she sighed, "but Saturday is our busiest day at my job. I really shouldn't, but I'll go there on Saturday morning and tell them I have an emergency and I'll be back in the afternoon and not to give my whole shift away."

I hated that she was making it very clear it was this big sacrifice, so I said, "I'll pay you for the hour I need you, Rosalia, I swear." And with Rosalia, money changes everything, so she said yes.

Our agreement was that she would meet me at the Thirty-fourth Street entrance to Macy's, but when I started walking toward the store, I could see she wasn't there.

"Please, please, Rosalia, don't mess this up for me," I was praying, waiting outside the store. I called Angie's number, hoping she was on a break or something and that maybe she could come down to the FeatureFace counter and—what? I could do a quickie makeup job on her and still get hired? Probably not.

But I had to go inside and change into my boots and at least scope out where the counter was so I wouldn't be late for my interview. "Rosalia," I said under my breath, "I will never forgive you for this!"

As soon as I got into the store, there was a guard, and I asked where the nearest men's room was. He mumbled something about the second floor or the basement, giving me this once-over that I didn't appreciate. *I mean, it's New York. Haven't you seen every kind of person there is in this city?* But I just followed his mumble and got on the escalator to the second floor. I don't do basements. Besides, I figured from the second floor I could get a helicopter view of the first floor and see where FeatureFace was.

The first floor was actually like Cosmetics Counters City. There was Mac and Chanel and Bobbi Brown's the Secret to Perfect Skin and Dolce & Gabbana and—yes, yes, yes!—there was FeatureFace! The whole area looked like there was an army of men and women in black guarding Cosmetics Counters City. They walked slowly through the aisles, staring out at the customers, or they stood behind the counters, glancing at themselves in the mirrors. Or saying something to one another as they patted or pulled on their hair, or ran their fingers over their stomachs as if they could make them tighter just by touching them. Some of them were armed with perfumes or creams. They were pacing the area, looking for a face or a hand or a neck like the glamour vampires. Once I saw the FeatureFace counter, I couldn't take my eyes off it. It had this big sign that spelled out "FeatureFace" in makeup mirror bulbs. Which one of those men was Valentino? The blond on blond on blond, or the black guy in the turtleneck with the choker on? That choker was severe. If the guy wearing it was Valentino, he would really appreciate my Stella McCartneys.

I found the men's room and took off my red sneakers. Pulled the Stellas out and pulled them up my thighs. I was *superb-ia* and I knew it. Just the five-inch heels alone were enough to make me feel like FeatureFace should be happy I was applying for the job. While I was checking my hair, this guy who'd come in at the same time I did stood next to me at the mirror for a minute. Then on his way out he said, "You go, boy!"

When I came out, I checked my cell. Four minutes to eleven and no message from Rosalia. *If she's not here, I may as well take these boots off and get right back on the train.* I was sweating. It was probably my imagination, but it felt like the Stella McCartneys were sweating too.

I went toward the escalator. Should I call Angie and beg her to come down to the first floor and help me? How could she say no? But then how could she risk losing her job by coming down to the first floor to have her makeup done? Probably not the best excuse she could offer her boss for leaving the linens department suddenly. "Excuse me, but I have to go down to the FeatureFace counter so my friend Carlos can do my makeup."

At the top of the escalator, I looked down at the first floor, toward the Cosmetics Counters City. I looked at the FeatureFace counter. Ohmygod! There was Rosalia, standing there with her coat over her arm in some very tight pants and a horrible orange and white fuzzy sweater that made her look like a big calico cat. And her hair was so humungous, it looked like she'd just escaped from a shock therapy session. But she was there! My model, Rosalia Duarte, sister of the very soon to be famous Carrlos Duarte, was there!

I raced down the escalator trying to look like I was

floating—but floating fast! I got to the FeatureFace counter without knowing how I got through the army of black uniforms and the thick screen of perfume and makeup.

"Hi," I said into Rosalia's neck, hugging her so hard, she laughed.

"Scared ya, didn't I? But I told ya I was coming, dork!"

I pulled myself together and looked at her. "I thought I told you to come without any makeup on!"

Rosalia frowned at me like I'd said, "I thought I told you to come without any clothes on!"

"Well, that wasn't going to happen," she snipped.

"May I help you with something today?" a voice chirped behind us.

I whirled around, and there was a girl with enough hair weave to compete in the Miss Black Rapunzel Contest. She was gorgeous, except for the green contacts, and I wanted to tell her she could do without about four feet of the weave, but instead I told her, "I have an interview with Valentino at eleven."

"Okay, hon," Miss Rapunzel chirped. She couldn't fling her hair because there was too much of it, hanging like a drape down the front and back of her black sheer blouse. (She had a tank top under it.) But she flung her shoulders anyway, which almost resembled flinging her hair. Off she went around the corner of the counter, and I took the time to take deep breaths and compose myself.

For some totally illogical reason, Rosalia started to pull at the horrible stretch pants she had strangling her butt. I mean, really, she was pulling her pants out of her hiny in front of the FeatureFace counter where I was trying to look like the next makeup superstar. I don't know if it was her nerves or what. But I had to ask her, "Rosalia, could you please!" And she stopped.

I could hear voices behind the counter, but I couldn't see who they belonged to. Just mumbling. More mumbling. Then Miss Rapunzel came back into view. "Valentino will be right out," she said cheerily.

"No, Valentino said he was busy and would come out as soon as he could," came this voice like the Wizard of Oz from behind the curtain. I was pretty sure from the sound of it that I'd better take a few more deep breaths.

Miss Rapunzel shrugged and laughed. She whispered, "Well, you heard him."

I smiled big because I wanted her to know I'd be fun to work with. "I'm Carlos, and this is my sis—this is Rosalia." I'd decided not to say that Rosalia was related to me, especially now with her in the stretch pants and the calico cat sweater. I wasn't ashamed of my sister. I was embarrassed that I didn't have a professional model and that the one I had looked like she was posing for a "Fashion Don't" column. Any other day but this one.

I saw his head first, then the top part of his body, then the bottom. In sections. He was a giraffe in a black V-neck sweater, black pants, and about thirty silver bracelets, fifteen on each arm.

He loped toward me in slow—very slow—motion. Can people be seven feet tall, with no fat on *any* part of their bodies? Pale, pale skin with two spots of pink on his cheeks that couldn't be real. His eyes were big black marbles with long black fringe framing them. His cinnamon hair stood out in every direction and still curled at the ends, so it was like a halo that shined under the fluorescent lights.

He was looking in our direction, but he didn't seem to be looking *at* us. He was looking over our heads, so when he stopped in front of us, I almost turned around to see what it was he was staring at.

"I'm Valentino," he announced. And he still wasn't looking at me or my sister.

"I'm Carrlos Duarte," I said as though I'd said it hundreds of times in professional situations, "and this is my model, Rosalia." I said it as though that was her professional name—Rosalia. Her first and only name.

His head tilted somewhat, but he still never focused on me. "Where have you worked before?"

I put my red book bag on the counter and quickly unzipped it. "I have my résumé here," I said, suddenly out of breath as though I'd run ten miles to get there.

"Just tell me where the last place you worked was. As a makeup artist." His voice sounded like a stapler, metallic and exact.

"Well, I go to school, so I haven't done it full-time. But I . . ." I was stalling, trying to think of a name to give him. Of course I'd rehearsed it, but I hadn't ever imagined the creature in front of me asking the question. "I worked on Saturdays and holidays at Bobby's, downtown."

"Bobby'sdowntown?" Still looking over the top of my head, he said it like it was one clearly made-up word. "And you say you're in school?"

"Yes, but I'm only applying for part-time right now. And Christmas."

"And other than this . . . Bobby's . . ." Valentino stared at my fake résumé like a bird had crapped on it. "I don't recognize any of these . . . places."

Just then Miss Rapunzel rushed up to Valentino. "Craig Denton is here, Val. He came in the other side. He asked where you were."

I immediately saw a change in Valentino, and I was thrilled to hear that Miss Rapunzel had cut his name to "Val," which I was sure I would someday. But who was Craig Denton?

"Our account executive is here today visiting. Couldn't have happened at a busier time," Valentino said, and sniffed. He put my résumé on the counter. "Why don't you get ready to work with your model, so I can see what you did at . . . Bobby's. I'll be back. Lissette will get you whatever you tell her you need."

As he turned to go, I saw the top of what must have been Craig Denton's shaved head somewhere behind the counter. And Valentino went to the person I guessed must have been his boss. "Oh," he said over his shoulder, "I want a Sunday brunch look. Then you will take it to a nighttime club look. I hope you learned how to do that at . . . Bobby's. And I'm hoping you weren't responsible for the makeup she's already wearing, because it's definitely *not* what we do at FeatureFace." I glared at my sister, who was busy rolling her horrifically made-up eyes at the man I hoped was going to be my future boss.

As soon as he was gone, Lissette Rapunzel asked softly, as though I was trying to light a brand-new gas oven with a book of matches, "Have you ever done this before?"

"Yes," I lied breezily. "Of course."

"You should just keep talking to me, telling me everything you're doing," she whispered. "When Valentino comes back, just keep talking. And don't forget to sell the product, baby!"

I turned Rosalia toward me like she was a life-size doll. "The first thing I'd like to do is give your face a good cleansing." I felt like I was doing an infomercial, which I guess I was. "We'll get rid of all this makeup, which I *didn't* put on"—I said loudly—"and we can start fresh! Lissette, do we have any of FeatureFace's Softwipes and their special Earth-friendly Gel Cleanser?" *Thank God for the Internet.* I'd done my homework, and I'd talk just loud enough to impress Lissette and so that Valentino could hear me a few feet away.

Lissette was giggling and had managed to start actually flinging her Rapunzel weave. She went to get the cleanser and the Softwipes.

"Why are you talking so friggin' loud?" Rosalia spat. "You're embarrassing me!"

"It's not *for* you," I spat back. "I know what I'm doing, so just please this once keep quiet!"

Lissette came back and put the cleanser and Softwipes on the counter next to me. "Thank you, Lissette. By the way, I love your hair."

I was used to using my fingers for everything. But when I started to rub the concealer under Rosalia's eye, Lissette made this sound at the back of her throat like she was choking, so I got the hint. "FeatureFace also has these wonderful brushes you can use. No one uses their fingers anymore," I said, and Lissette couldn't stop herself from laughing.

A few minutes later I could hear Valentino talking to Craig Denton as I got to Rosalia's eye shadow. They were coming toward us. I was feeling so good, I got even louder. "Now I'm going to use FeatureFace's incredible Perfect Pink as the base. You can see it's a subtle, more neutral pink—

which my customers love—and we're using it to hold our color down. And we'll put a deeper, richer pink on top. I'm going to put a nice medium brown in the crease, keeping it subtle. Remember, it's your daytime look, so subtlety is the key." I stole that last bit directly from a *Vogue* article I'd read last fall about daytime makeup. It was hysterical, me telling Rosalia how subtlety was key. I knew she couldn't wait to get out of there so she could put her Egyptian mummy makeup back on.

Valentino and Craig Denton were now right behind Lissette! They'd stopped talking, and both of them were watching me like I was the eleven o'clock news, Special Edition.

"The thing that's so great about FeatureFace's shadows is how they create so much dimension with such little effort!" I had no idea what I was saying, really. It was everything I'd ever studied mixed with every ad and commercial for makeup I'd ever seen. I just kept gushing about FeatureFace.

"You're very good for someone so young. How long have you been working for us?" I kept brushing Rosalia's eyelids, not able to speak. Was this guy really speaking to me? *How long have you been working for us?*

"He doesn't." Valentino sounded dry, but not as dry as he had when he'd been talking to me. Not at all. "This is an interview. I'm not sure he has as much experience as we'd like."

"Oh, come on," Craig Denton said, and I could tell he was smiling even though I was too nervous to look at him. "He obviously knows what he's doing. And he's definitely a good salesman."

"Yes," Valentino said in this tone that could have been agreeing to having his cavities drilled.

"I'll be curious to see what this looks like when you're finished—what is your name?"

"Carrlos Duarte," I said, wishing I could have announced it in the voice I used when I was daydreaming something like this was happening.

"Well, if I'm still here, Lissette, you come get me."

"Absolutely, Craig," Lissette bubbled. I could have hugged her.

"I'm not sure you *will* still be here, Craig." Valentino sighed. "He's going *very* slowly. As far as I'm concerned, he should have finished the first look already. Our customers don't have the luxury of sitting around all day—"

"You know, Val, speed is something that comes with time. When he's been doing it for as long as you have"—Craig Denton chuckled—"I'm sure he'll be as fast as you are." Valentino's mouth did this puckering thing that looked like he was tasting the words "for as long as you have," and they didn't taste good at all.

"Fine," Valentino snapped. "When he's finally finished the first look, Lissette, let us know." Then he huffed to Craig Denton, "If you want to see the totals, they're this way." And they went around the corner to another part of the FeatureFace counter.

As soon as they'd gone, Rosalia squealed, "Ooo, Carlos!"

"Do you know how fabulous that is?" Lissette's hair was really flying now.

"Who is he?" I asked.

"Craig Denton, the Manager of Retail Operations. And he oversees all the FeatureFace retail outlets in the city.

He started on the floor, then was a counter manager like Valentino, then got promoted to MRO."

"And does it matter if he likes what I'm doing?"

"Let's put it this way: If he likes what he sees, Valentino would have to explain why he *didn't* hire you."

"Then why is Valentino being soooo . . ." I wasn't sure I should say exactly what I was thinking. But I really didn't understand why, if I was good, he wasn't being any friendlier.

"If you get the job, honey, we can go have tea and I'll give you all the dirt. But for now just work fast so you can get employed!"

I started to paint Rosalia's face like we were on the subway tracks, a train was coming, and neither one of us could escape till her makeup was done. From eyeliner I went to mascara, and from mascara I went to lipstick moisturizer, and as I finished her lip gloss, I told Lissette, "All right, go tell 'em they can come take a look!"

In the few minutes Lissette was gone, Rosalia wiggled and tried not to scream out loud, and I checked and rechecked what I'd done on her. Valentino would have to admit it wasn't at all the girl he'd seen when I started. The only evidence was the calico cat sweater, the nightmare stretch pants, and the hair, straight out of *Grease* meets Miss Puerto Rico Beauty Pageant 1980.

When Lissette led Val and his boss back, I pretended I was just putting on some finishing touches with the lip brush.

"See, I was right. The kid has some talent!" Craig Denton stood there in front of Rosalia, and I got a good look at his suit. *Someday,* I thought. *I'll own one of those. Only I'll still add some me to it somehow and it will look even better.*

"You know, Craig," Valentino drawled, "this is still only half of what is required. Usually, as you know, there are *two* looks—"

"Yes, I do. And since it seems to be taking us a considerable amount of time to look at your totals, I'll no doubt be here when his second look is done." He turned to Lissette. "Come get us, would you?"

Valentino was boiling. "It will take us no time at all, I'm sure. Juan—"

"Carlos!" I shot my correction back at him. *Don't even try that with me.*

Valentino looked shocked at my tone. "Carlos. You have twenty minutes to complete the nighttime look. Thank you." He turned and floated away as though his tasseled loafers never hit the floor.

But I heard Craig Denton say to Valentino, "I don't know if I could have done it that well when I started, and certainly not with any speed. And I thought I was damn good. What about you?"

"Actually, yes, I thought I was very good," Valentino purred. "And you must have thought so too, Craig. You hired me."

Rosalia sucked her teeth loud enough for everybody to have heard it. They probably heard it across the room. *Please, Rosalia. Control yourself, girl. This is not the time!*

It was exactly eighteen minutes later when Valentino and Mr. Denton came back. I remember because Lissette announced when it was seventeen minutes, and I still hadn't put any lip gloss on Rosalia. When I heard the two of them coming, I decided to leave it rather than look like I hadn't finished on time.

"I see you managed," Mr. Denton said, "and from what I can see, I'm pretty impressed."

I was just about to thank him when Valentino said, "Well, I'm *still* concerned about how slow he is. If there was a line here on a Saturday, we'd be in big trouble. And I won't always be here to give him a time limit."

Mr. Denton said calmly, "I understand your concern, Valentino."

"And, frankly, I don't think the references are quite up to our standards."

Mr. Denton looked at me from head to toe. I couldn't have been more grateful at that moment for my Stella McCartneys. I was tempted to ease casually into a ballet position that showed them off more, but I thought it might be too much.

"Do you have a portfolio, Carlos?"

"Of course, Mr. Denton," I said, reaching over to the counter to get my bag. I heard Mr. Denton chuckle, and I knew both my Stellas and my red vinyl had scored.

Opening to my pictures, I said, "Obviously, this is just a sample of my work." I suddenly wished I had thirty more photos, with layouts from *Bazaar* or *Teen Vogue* or at least a Kmart catalogue!

Valentino sniped, "There's not a lot of variety. Looks like they were all done by the same photographer. Probably at the same shoot." I thought about a TV commercial where a little boy eats glue and can't open his mouth to speak. That's what I fantasized about the mean giraffe in the V-neck sweater and the thirty bracelets.

"Still, it's good work," Mr. Denton said. He looked from Rosalia's picture to her. "Is this the same model?"

"Yes," we both said. Actually, Rosalia kind of shouted "Yeah!" and grinned. I flashed her a look that said, *Don't say. One. Single. Word.*

Mr. Denton stepped back and stared at me. I stared right back. *Go on. Do it. Hire me. It's the best decision you'll ever make!*

He said, "I think this is someone we want to give a chance, Val. Just as you were given a chance . . . and I was given a chance before you."

With the five of us in the same small area, it seemed like there wasn't a sound.

Finally Mr. Denton broke the silence. "What's the worst that could happen? I'm sure our young friend here knows that if he can't keep up, we can't afford to keep him on salary. Don't you, Carlos?"

I turned to both of them. "I know I can keep up."

There was another big, long silence. I knew I'd said all I could say, and I was hoping Rosalia had sense enough to keep her mouth shut. Lissette had made herself practically invisible, and all I could concentrate on were Valentino and Craig Denton. *Please, God. Please.*

"Well, if you're that impressed, Craig," Valentino drawled.

"I am," Mr. Denton said, and I put my hand on Rosalia's knee and squeezed it hard. Rosalia put hers over mine and clamped it like she was Mickey Rourke in *The Wrestler*.

"Then, I guess it's settled." Valentino looked like he was at a fancy dinner party and hated everything on his plate, but all he could do was smile and try to get some of it down.

"Welcome," Craig Denton said to me, and put out his hand. I wanted to hug him, but I wasn't *that* crazy.

"Thank you very much, Mr. Denton."

"Please don't call me Mr. Denton. It makes me feel about seventy-five years old. And, just so you know, you are now working for the most dynamic cosmetics firm in the industry," he told me in this honey-dripping baritone. "Not only do we have one of the strongest retail lines in the world, but we also have a huge celebrity client base. Once you get some real education on the line, I'm sure you'll be very impressed."

"I'm impressed already," I told him. I was trying to imitate his baritone honey drip. I gave him my biggest Carrlos Duarte, celebrity-in-training smile. And I could see Valentino, the giraffe in the V-neck sweater, rolling his big black marble eyes up toward the Macy's chandeliers.

chapter 1

I was in shock. I could hardly think. And Rosalia kept shrieking, "Man, Carlos, I can't believe it! I can't friggin' believe it!"

I was trying to get her away from the counter before it became really obvious, if it hadn't been before, that she was no professional model—she was my sister who thought it was a miracle I just got hired to do what I'd done on her and her dolls for years.

Valentino told me, "I'll call you with the date you're going to start working." He said it like it hurt. I thanked him so much for giving me the opportunity—yeah, right. Craig Denton had already disappeared, like he'd been some magic suntanned genie.

When me and Rosalia were going through the revolving doors on the way out—I'm not gonna lie—I remember realizing that I still had on the Stella McCartneys. It was just for a second, but I did think of it. But I couldn't go back into the store to take them off. Not then. Not when all the cameras in my head were watching *Carlos Duarte, Newly Hired Macy's Makeup Artist, and His Model-Sister, Rosalia, Leaving the World Famous Department Store.* How could I stop, go back into the men's room, and change into a pair of dirty sneakers at a moment like that?

I went with Rosalia from the store to the subway practically without realizing how I got there. We kept going over all the details, with Rosalia teasing, "Carlos, if it hadn't been for *me* being the model, you wouldn't have done that good!"

"Uh-huh," I said sarcastically, but to tell the truth, I was really glad that she was the one who'd been there. She was family, and it meant a lot to me that she was my sister and was proud of me.

"I have to go right to work and hope I'm not fired," she said. That's what brought me back to reality.

"You won't be, hon," I told her. "Today is too special. Nothing can go wrong, I swear."

At Fourteenth Street, when Rosalia got off the train, I gave her a kiss on the cheek. "You're right," I told her. "If I hadn't had you there, it would never have gone the way it did." Rosalia did the Cabbage Patch dance and sang, "Yougonnabefamous, yougonnabefamous" on the platform until the subway door closed.

At Eighth Street, when I got off the train, I started daydreaming again about every detail of what happened at the store. I walked all the way to the end of the platform, talking to myself, repeating everything that Craig Denton had said about me to Valentino.

When I got to the bottom of the stairs, I looked up and saw Danny. Behind him were his two friends from Burrito Take-Out Village coming down toward me.

"Hi," I said softly to Danny. He didn't say anything. I started up the stairs. I tripped on something and glanced down to see what it was. It looked like a rusty curtain rod. I moved aside so that the guys could pass. I looked up again at Danny. So he was going to ignore me. He was my sister's boyfriend, but he wasn't even going to try to force a fake "hi" just for her sake.

As they got closer, I could smell liquor on them. I don't drink, so I couldn't tell you exactly what it was, but I can tell you if how badly it stunk was any test of how much they'd had, they'd had a lot.

One of them said, "Oooooh, Carrrloooss!" in this really girly voice. Danny was already next to me. One of the others was standing above me on the stairs. He spit down at me. I backed up, trying to get away. I fell, and the spit hit the front of my jacket anyway. Danny and the other kid started laughing.

I was half lying, half sitting on the subway stairs glaring up at my sister's boyfriend. I wasn't scared. I was mad.

It wasn't as though I didn't know them. I knew where they worked, and I could bring a cop there in a second. Was he crazy? Were they all crazy? Danny reached down. I froze. Danny grabbed the curtain rod and handed it to his friend. It was like he was giving him instructions that didn't need to be said out loud. The guy took the rod and pulled it up one of my boots, scratching the smooth black leather from the toe all the way up the thigh. I grabbed the end of it and tried to jump up and get out of his way, but I wasn't fast enough. "You stupid piece of garbage!" I screamed. "You piece of crap!"

Someone was on their way up the stairs. The guys all ran past me, laughing and calling my name. "Carrrloooss! Carrrloooss!" I only knew one of their names—Danny's—but it didn't matter. I could see all of their faces, and I knew where to find them. And I wasn't sure exactly what I'd do. But I had to do something. I looked down at the ruined boots I should have taken off like I'd sworn I would. I wiped the spit off the front of my jacket with my sleeve.

At home I tried to think of how I could fix the scratch before I took the boots back to Soraya. But when I saw how deep and long it was, I realized there was no way anybody was gonna pay three hundred dollars for those boots any-more, Stella McCartneys or not. And besides that, I would have done anything not to face Soraya. What could I say? I wore them out of the store like I'd promised I wouldn't, and then I got them destroyed by a friend of my sister's boyfriend?

And that's exactly what I *did* say to Soraya. It didn't make sense for me to tell a lie, because there wasn't a lie that would make any sense. No matter how it happened, acci-dentally or on purpose, the boots were ruined. So I just told Soraya the truth. I finished by saying, "All I can do is say if you give me enough time, I can pay for them. But it will be a while, even with my new job."

Soraya couldn't have cared less about my new job, which was understandable, since now she was worried about los-ing hers.

"What do you think this is, Carlos? We don't do layaway! It's not that kind of store. You come back here with ruined merchandise that I let you take out of here, and you expect me to put you on a payment plan? You're living in a bigger fantasy world than I thought! I trusted you!"

"I'm really sorry, Soraya. I know I let you down, and I know you probably hate me. But all I can do is offer to pay for the boots. And if I had three hundred dollars right now, I'd give it to you. But I don't."

"So all you can do is apologize—I got it. Now, could you please leave the store, Carlos? I have customers."

She said it like she didn't know me and I was loitering. And I couldn't blame her. I just hoped she wouldn't be fired because of me. Especially now that I had just gotten the job of my dreams.

I walked out of Tokyo Jo's feeling like I'd done far more damage to our friendship than the burrito boy had done to the freakin' Stella McCartneys. I glanced down at my jacket and remembered how excited Soraya had been when she'd told me she could sell it to me for so much less because it was a little faded. Today some guy had spit on it. And in a way I felt like I'd done the same to my friendship with Soraya.

Chapter 8

Before I could say anything, before I could even begin, Rosalia came home from work and started. "I just had the worst afternoon of my life, the worst! It started off just fine with you, Carlos, and then I get to work and I'm in a perfectly good mood. And then they tell me Danny, Juan, and Oscar are all fired."

She didn't wait for me to say anything. "There was money missing from the cash register, and Tina, the girl who was working for me, said she had just counted an hour before that and she wasn't short, so Miguel goes off and fires Danny, Juan, and Oscar on the spot. I call Danny every chance I get and he's not answering his phone." She plopped down onto the couch with her face to the ceiling and her hands over her face.

Ma said, "Well, maybe he's not answering because he feels guilty," and Rosalia went nuts. "Thanks, Ma. Thank you very much. I know you don't like him and you don't even know him. So now he's a thief?"

"I'm just saying, why won't he answer his phone and talk to you if he's so innocent?"

And that's when I knew I wasn't going to bring up what happened with Danny and these other two guys whose names I didn't know before. But I did ask Rosalia to repeat them, because when I did decide to do whatever I was going to do about them, I'd at least have all of their freaking names.

"I'm not saying they're thieves, Rosalia, but I do agree with Ma that it's weird the guy won't return your phone calls if he doesn't have anything to hide."

And when Rosalia gave me a dirty look and said, "How can you be so unsympathetic? You got everything you wanted today, didn't you?" I thought *I really should just tell her right now.* But then she started crying and said, "It's like you always say, Carlos. You're gonna be famous and have money and a decent life. And I'm always gonna be stuck with some guy that people think is a thief or a drug addict or some other dirtbag."

And, yes, I did think he was trash. And that's exactly what I wanted to tell my sister, and fill her in on why. But I didn't. Because, yeah, the day started out great and I couldn't be happier about getting hired by FeatureFace. But I also probably lost a friend because I was a big liar and I didn't keep my word. So I couldn't make myself tell my sister that her boyfriend and his friends attacked me and they probably did steal the money at her job. I just couldn't.

But I *did* tell Angie. She said I should go to the police and report what she kept calling "an assault." When she started calling the curtain rod a deadly weapon, I told her she should get a job writing for *Law and Order.*

I'm not going to report it," I told her. "If those pigs are arrested for stealing from that stupid burrito stand, it will be justice enough. I hope the cops put them in the Tombs for seventy-five years."

"Yeah," Angie said. "That's if the owner even presses charges."

"How could he not press charges?" I thought she was being ridiculous.

"People get fired for stealing all the time," Angie said like she was the theft authority, "and people don't press charges. How much could they have stolen from a burrito take-out register? A hundred dollars? I betcha nothing happens, Carlos. And didn't you say Danny was one of the cooks and the others were just kitchen helpers? Then he could blame it on them and keep his job. You watch."

"I'd die," I told her. "Seriously. I'd die."

But I didn't die. For the next few days I waited for Rosalia to come home from work and say her boss was pressing charges against Danny. Instead she texted me one day and told me exactly what Angie had predicted. Her text said, "thank Gd. D tld Miguel he dint steal the mny. he sys one of the otr giys did it. Mig sd d cld cme bac!!! im sooo hppy."

I guess that day there was good news for both of us. Lissette called from Macy's and told me Valentino wanted me to come to work the next Saturday. I called Angie and told her.

We went to the Thai Palace on Fourteenth Street to celebrate. She almost ruined the night by bugging me to tell Rosalia what happened in the subway station. "I always thought you had more guts than to let something like this happen to you and not do anything!"

"It's extenuating circumstances and you're about to ruin our celebration dinner, Angie."

I tried to bring the focus of the night back to where it should be—on me and my future as a makeup star.

"Angie," I said, "do you remember the first time you dared me to put on a full face of makeup to go to the movies, and I did?"

"Of course." She laughed. "We got into a fight because people kept staring, and you said, 'What did you expect? I'm beautiful.' And I said you overdid it because you knew people would stare."

"Then you said," I reminded Angie, "'Well, you must have been putting on makeup since you were born.' And I said, 'Angie girl, I've been putting makeup on the fat boy for a very long time.' We stood there in the movie line laughing until your makeup started running, and I said, 'See, Ange, that would never happen to me! That's why I'm the expert,' and we laughed some more."

I had Angie cracking up at the memory. I told her, "Well, now someone is paying the fat boy to put makeup on *other* people. And it's only the beginning!"

But she still couldn't get over the story about Danny and the run-in on the subway stairs. "You're gonna be sorry if you don't do something about it, Carlos. Just trust me. I can feel it."

And I told my friend, "Angie, please just eat your fried rice and think only good thoughts! Think that one day I'll be rich enough to buy this place. We can eat all the spring rolls we want and drink all the Thai iced tea we want, and every time something good happens to us, we can fill the place with our friends and family. We can have Thai Christmas dinners and Thanksgivings and New Year's Eve parties."

But the whole time we sat there, it was true I never stopped picturing the guy standing over me, dragging that curtain rod up my boot and spitting on me.

Chapter 9

Don't get me wrong. I love kids, and the whole day care center thing was perfect. Just enough hours to give me some money, and it didn't interfere at all with school because it certainly wasn't tiring. And I thought that maybe if I was around little kids, I could influence them a little not to be crummy people like a lot of adults I knew.

But I have to admit that when even the possibility of working for FeatureFace came up, I started thinking how my whole career was coming together. It seemed like all my dreams for my future were starting to materialize before I'd even graduated high school. So I was pretty sure if it happened, I'd resign from my position as assistant counselor at the Lower East Side Day Care Center. I even kidded with one of the teachers, Masai, about how I wanted her to be sure and tell a couple of the fathers, who were so nervous about me being around their kids, that I'd left to be a makeup artist at Macy's. You should see how some of the fathers looked at me, like they were afraid to have their kids left alone with me. I also told her to tell them I said they should tell their wives to be sure and come see me for a special discount.

Just days after Lissette called and told me to come to work the next Saturday, Ma met me outside the day care center when I got off work. She looked like one of my little kids when their parents don't show up.

It was dark out, around seven. I get out at seven, but there were always kids still left for one reason or another. One of my favorite kids, Bickel, left with his mother, and then when I turned around, he was back. His mother said, "Bickel wants to talk to you." So I went over to him, hoping it wasn't something horrible, although I couldn't imagine how it could be.

"Carlos," he said in his foggy little voice, "there's a lady outside who looks like you. I think it's your mother."

So even though he'd never even seen my mother, I thought there had to be something to what he said.

I went to the door and looked out. Ma was standing on the stoop of the center, which is in one of those ugly New York brick buildings that look like they're part of a housing project, even if they aren't. Except this one was.

Ma was a few feet away from the door. But she was right under the light, which wasn't the most flattering for anybody, much less Ma, who looked like she'd either been caught in the rain—and it hadn't been raining—or she'd been crying. And Ma was not a crier.

Opening the center door, I asked her, "What's going on, Ma?"

She said in a dry voice, "I'm waiting for you."

I knew my mother and I knew when something was wrong. Not only was it weird that she was there, but just the look of her was sending off alarm signals. So I pulled the door behind me and stepped out. Little Bickel was still looking back, and said, "Bye, Carlos, bye!" and I got that he could sense something was wrong, like he was a little antenna who picked up the airwaves. I called good-bye to him and went over to my mother.

"Why do you look like that?" I asked Ma. "What's happening?"

She didn't look at me. "I'm laid off. Whatever that means."

I could not believe what she said. I understood layoffs for corporations and big businesses and I guess every other job situation, but . . . the cleaner's? How do you get laid off from managing a cleaners? Is that possible?

"Well, what did he say it means?" I asked her.

"He didn't say what it meant. I said, 'Dominic, if I'm fired, please tell me. 'Cause I don't know what you're saying. And if I have to look for a job, I gotta know. But he just said, 'We're not makin' enough money for me to keep you on full-time.'

"So," Ma said, "I asked him, 'What about part-time?' And he said, 'I can't afford you right now, Maria. I gotta make some serious changes in order to keep this place open.'"

"Did you ask him when you could go back?" I had to believe eventually she was going to say something that would make it not as awful as it sounded.

She shrugged. "He said he didn't know anything. He said, 'Of course, as soon as I can, I'll call you. I know where to find you.'"

"God, Ma, I'm sorry," I told her, and when another kid came out of the center with her mother, I realized my plans for quitting this job had just gotten flushed down the toilet. How could I quit *any* job when my mother just got laid off? We were already living in an apartment building that looked like it was built when New York first became a city. But when I leave school, start to work full-time, and get filthy freakin' rich, I'm gonna move Ma out. She won't even be in the same neighborhood. But if she is, she'll be telling Dominic, Mr. Quik Clean & Press, that all he can do for her is Quik Clean & Press her furs. But then that sounded like a not so good idea.

"There's nothing to be sorry about. I just gotta find another job."

I remembered that she said she was waiting for me. But I knew it couldn't be to just tell me this crummy news. It wasn't like her.

"You said . . ."

"I need ya to come help me carry my things. I been there so long, I got a lotta stuff there, plus I asked him could I have some stuff that's just been sittin' there. You know, stuff that nobody claimed. I figured if you don't want it, you could just throw it out. But since you're startin' a new job and all . . ."

I looked at my mother under the stoop light of the day care center. She had dark brown hair with some gray in it. I hated the dyed color, but she wouldn't pay money for good dye, and she only went to the hairdresser when she had a wedding or an important funeral to go to. At least wasn't red or bleached blond like a lot of other Spanish women her age—forty-three. I guess they thought if you're going to change your hair color, why go to another shade of brown? But my mother seemed pretty satisfied just not to have all gray hair. She dyed it brown with auburn highlights—Kissed by Auburn, it's called. Right now she needed a dye job bad. Her face was a little lined, but usually I didn't think you could tell she was forty-three.

That night, though, she definitely looked her age, except her eyes looked like a tired little girl's. She looked disappointed, as though she just found out someone very important to her told her a big fat lie.

"Can you come inside while I get my jacket and bag?" I asked her. But she said, "I'm sorry to bother you. I thought you were getting off now."

"I am," I told her. "But I have to get my jacket and tell them I'm leaving."

I went back inside, and the teachers asked me what was wrong. "It'll be fine," I told them. My mother would have lied down on the day care stoop and died if I ever told them what she called her "personal business," which included just about everything in her life, from how long she was married to what her middle name was, to whether she believed in God or not, to what shade of nail polish she wore.

I grabbed my jacket and bag, and Masai said, "Come here, boy," and hugged me. "You have a good night," she said, looking me in the eye.

"Thanks, Masai." I yelled my good-byes to the rest of the staff, and I went out the door.

Quik Clean & Press was only a few blocks away, but it seemed to take us twice as long as it ordinarily would, because neither me nor Ma said anything. I think it would have been so much easier and more dignified if we had just got Ma's stuff and not some stuff she wanted to bring home to me and Rosalia because no one else wanted it. In all the times she'd brought stuff home, and she'd done it for the whole six years she'd worked there, I've kept maybe two things. The rest was so ugly, it was pretty obvious to me why the people who owned it decided they may as well leave it at the cleaner's. Rosalia's kept more because she's greedy, and also because she has really bad taste. But I really wished Ma had more pride than to take a pity package home with her when Dominic really should have given her some kind of bonus for being such a good worker for so long and for him giving her such a messed-up break.

When we got to the cleaners, Dominic had most of the lights off already. "I wasn't sure you were coming back," he said to Ma. He didn't even say "Hello, Carlos" or anything. He didn't look at me. Maybe he was embarrassed, and he should have been.

"I told you I was coming back. I wouldn't leave my things here." I knew Ma would be pissed if she knew I could hear the hurt in her voice. She was trying to be casual, and maybe Dominic didn't hear the hurt, but I did. That was the thing with Ma. If you couldn't tell what she was feeling about something, it was because you didn't want to.

She came from the back with this big garbage bag. She handed it to me, and it was heavy enough to have two men inside it. "Ma," I said quietly, "are you sure we need to take all of this?"

Now she had her arms full with another bag. "Part of it is mine. What you don't want, you don't want."

I walked to the door of the cleaner's. I either wanted Dominic to tell her that he'd changed his mind or that he'd call her very soon, or I wanted to go. I didn't want to be there with her looking like she did and not be able to say or do anything about it.

"So you'll let me know if things get better?" Ma said to him.

"Yeah," he said, and maybe I wasn't being fair to him, but I thought he sounded like he couldn't wait for us to leave so he could lock up and walk away thinking, *Well, that's done.*

A block away from Quik Clean & Press, Ma said to me, "What do you think?"

I couldn't even guess what she meant. And I definitely didn't want to risk saying something idiotic tonight.

"About what?" I asked her.

"You think he'll ever call?"

"I don't know, Ma." I tried immediately to think of something better to come up with. Something that would make her feel better.

"It doesn't matter. It won't be soon enough," she said, and sighed. "I gotta start lookin' for something right away."

"I'm even more glad about getting the FeatureFace job now," I said. "I'll have the day care center and FeatureFace. It won't be a lot, but I can give you more to help out."

"You're supposed to be saving for college with that money, Carlos. It's not a lot as it is. And putting makeup on people can't be a whole lot more."

Now my feelings were hurt. "It's money, Ma. It's more than I *was* making. And you don't know what could happen from it. I could do magazine work, maybe. Or a movie."

Ma stopped right there and looked at me like she was gonna hit me. "You finish your school. And you get your ass into college. This is not a TV show. You are not gonna be famous working at Macy's, and you are not gonna get rich working on the weekends. So you work and you come home and you study and you graduate and you go to college. You got it?"

My jaw tightened, but I didn't answer. I hated it when she stopped in the middle of the sidewalk to tell me off, which she's done since me and Rosalia could barely walk. It didn't matter where we were or who we were with. If she was gonna let us have it, she was gonna let us have it.

Ma started walking again. We didn't say anything to each other until we were almost home. When we got to our apartment building, she looked at me. "You know that bottle of wine Dominic gave me for Christmas?"

"Yeah," I answered.

"You think it's any good?"

"How would I know? I don't drink wine." And it was the truth. Basically. I mean I didn't drink it enough to know whether a wine was a good wine, just if it tasted crummy or not. And I knew that if it tasted really crummy, it was probably cheap.

"I think I'll open it tonight and have a glass. Or two." And then Ma laughed. "And tomorrow I'll get up and think about gettin' a new job."

I've dragged the garbage bag of other people's clothes to the fourth-floor landing when I told her, "You know, it may not be much, but I can still help with the money."

Ma shot me a look, but before she could start on me again, I said, "And it doesn't mean I won't go to college." But of course the plan was exactly what I've always said. I'm going to work for magazines and movies and television.

And move her out of this falling-down building.

When we got to the sixth floor, I dropped the garbage bag in the hallway in front of our door. Ma said to me, "Dominic says he has a brother who has a cleaner's farther uptown. He's gonna give him a call and see if he needs somebody. Pray he does."

"I will, Ma. I will."

Chapter 10

Walking into school, I heard this voice I didn't recognize at first. "Carlos?"

When I turned, I still didn't see where the voice was coming from. Or maybe it was just new to me, hearing him call out to me at all. I lowered my sunglasses a bit, to get a better look at who was trailing in, but there were about four kids I talked to in the whole school, including Angie, and I swear I didn't see any of them.

Inside, on my way down the hall, I was thinking about Ma and hoping she got the job at the cleaner's that Dominic's brother owned. I was also thinking that it sucked that I'd promised to call her after my first class to ask her if she got it. If she did, I'd only be happy because she was happy and—let's face it—it was money. But if she didn't, I knew she'd be upset and worried and I'd have about three minutes before my next class to say—what? "That's okay, you'll find something" or "Why don't you check the papers to see what else is out there?" Honestly, I could wait either way for the news.

"Carlos."

I actually jumped and made this little shriek.

"Sorry I scared you. I was calling you outside, and you turned around and looked right at me."

"I did? I'm sorry, Gleason. I did hear somebody calling me. I just wasn't sure where it was coming from." He had on the tightest red T-shirt with a faded black-and-white photo of Jimi Hendrix on it. Black skinny jeans and black work boots open, with the laces hanging like he'd just gotten out of bed and slipped them on at the last minute. It was the gray eyes, though, that got me every time.

"I wanted to ask you something," he said.

I could have made a thousand cracks, but, as my English teacher Ms. Gillespie says, I refrained. "Anything." I smiled at what I wasn't saying, and stared at him from behind my dark glasses.

"I'm thinking about putting some of the photographs I took for you in a show I got in, and I wanted to get your okay."

"A show? You're gonna put them in a photography show? When is it? Of course it's okay! What are you, crazy? *You* took them—they're as much yours as they are mine! You certainly don't have to ask me!"

I was completely stunned. I knew he was in the photography club, and I also knew he took great photographs, but I didn't think he was that serious or that ambitious. But then, I also didn't know him half as well as I wanted to.

He pulled his hand slowly through his curls, kind of tugging at them. It was *beyond sexy*—the boy was truly dangerous. "I only got a chance to take the model shots because you asked me to," he said. "But when the guy who put me in the show saw all my pictures, he said I should definitely include them. He said it showed that I had a good eye for more than rock concerts and bands."

"And is this your first show?"

"Yeah. This . . . uh . . . friend of mine, Gabrielle, knows somebody who works in this gallery, and they were doing this show that's supposedly new talent that they think is gonna be big someday. Gabs got her friend to show her boss, the guy who runs the gallery, my stuff . . ." Gleason shrugged shyly. "I guess he thought I fit that description."

I wanted to tell Gleason Kraft just how many descriptions I thought he fit, but again, I used willpower.

"So am I invited to the opening?" I asked him. "Or is it only for celebrities and the press?" Of course, in my mind, I was definitely a celebrity even if only Angie and me knew it.

"Yeah, sure you are, if you want to. I don't really know anything about the opening yet. But if I can invite people, then, sure."

"What do you mean *if* you can invite people? It's your show, isn't it?"

"Naw," he said, laughing. "I just told you, it's a *group* show. There are about seven other people, I think."

"I'm really happy for you, Gleason. And I'm glad I asked you to do my pictures."

It was then that two of his rocker buddies called him, and it was as though the Gleason I was talking to disappeared and his stand-in took his place. Except to me, it wasn't that good a stand-in because even though he looked like Gleason, everything about him was different. He sounded different, his face wasn't as alive and warm as Gleason's, the way he was standing changed. It was odd, and it was a little sad, I thought. Because I'd never seen the Gleason I was talking to before, really. I'd seen glimpses of him when we were doing the shoots, but today talking about his show, he was all there. And then suddenly he was gone.

"So I'll let you know about the show and stuff," he said, backing away toward his friends.

"I hope so," I told him. "Don't forget, if it wasn't for me . . ." It was a jerky thing to say and I felt like a big idiot. He'd already said he was asking me if he could put the pictures in the show because he knew I was responsible for him taking them. Now the last impression of me he had was that I was a butthead. I could hold my breath for an invitation now.

But don't think for a minute that I didn't start to daydream about it right then in the hall. I didn't have all the details, but I definitely could see me getting out of my limo and calmly walking though the paparazzi. I couldn't tell you what I was wearing, because it was such an instant fantasy—who had time to plan—but I could just feel that I looked *beyond excellent*, and when I came into the gallery, Gleason came right over and grabbed a glass of champagne from the nearest waiter and said, "I didn't think you were coming," in this voice that sounded like Jeremy Irons. And I smiled and looked over his shoulder, which was hard because Gleason had on a tuxedo with his red T-shirt and I probably could have just stared at him. But the photographs were billboard-size and underneath were these signs that said, THESE PHOTOS ARE DEDICATED TO CARRLOS DUARTE, BECAUSE WITHOUT HIM THEY WOULDN'T EXIST.

"Carlos?"

I heard Angie, and I really didn't want to come out of the

daydream. Especially to be in the reality of Sojourner Truth/ John F. Kennedy Freedom High School at eight thirty on a Tuesday morning.

"Hi, hon."

"What was Gleason talking about?"

"Oh, that." I pulled my glasses down onto my nose to look at her with raised eyebrows, and I said, "Angie, I don't think I realized it before, but I think I have a . . . a thing for Gleason Kraft."

At this point Angie got very, very loud. She screamed with laughter like she was naked and there were a hundred little men tickling her in all the right places.

"What is so funny, Angie? You're embarrassing me!"

"I can't believe you're trying to tell me you didn't realize you had a thing for Gleason Kraft!"

Now I'm paranoid that she made an announcement to the entire student body. She may as well have been handing out leaflets.

"Would you keep your voice down, pleeeez! I really don't get what the big joke is!"

"There is no joke. I just can't believe that as smart as you're supposed to be, how come you're the last to get that you have a thing for Gleason Kraft!"

And I couldn't answer her. Because what she didn't know was that what I was really saying was I never *admitted* to myself that I was infatuated with Gleason Kraft before. But the fact was, the Gleason I saw *before* he disappeared, the Gleason who called to me and told me about his show, made me think that maybe I might get a chance to . . . to what? I didn't know. But the *chance* part. That's what was important.

Chapter 11

I thought when I left the human resources office of Macy's and went down to the first floor as an official FeatureFace employee, the chandeliers would get brighter or the FeatureFace sign would start chiming or something. But neither of those things happened. What actually happened was that Lissette announced to me, "Val's gonna be late as usual. Only I'm not supposed to tell you he's late, of course. But I am supposed to show you where everything is and in between you should jump right in and see if you can make any sales."

And that was the name of the game—SALES.

Lissette explained, "I don't know where else you've worked doing this"—and I could tell there was big question mark in her voice—"but for this company it's about customer satisfaction and sales. From the time you start applying makeup, you are letting the customer know—I don't care whether it's man, woman, child, or chimp—you are letting them know what the product is and encouraging them to buy it, buy several, because you are showing them right then and there that it works for them!"

I was nodding and nodding, and I wanted to laugh because she was so loud and so funny and kept tossing her hair around like she was auditioning to be a Beyoncé backup dancer.

"We've had so-called makeup artists come in here, and they think it's all about putting on the makeup. So they spend hours and hours putting on the makeup and chit-chatting and at the end the customer gets up, looks in the mirror, sometimes says "Thank you"—occasionally they don't even say that—and then, gone! And what have we sold? Nothing! So the customer got a free makeup consultation and they're going off to lunch or dinner or back to work and the makeup artist has worked her or his butt off, and no sale! And do you think Valentino is happy about that? No! Because at the end of the day, Craig Denton, the manager of retail operations, wants those numbers, and Valentino has to give 'em up. We are all responsible, but Valentino's butt is on the line!"

"I understand," I told her. I was glad she was telling me this and not Valentino, because it made me understand what I didn't know about the business and, more important, what Val wanted from me.

Lissette stopped her training to help a customer. I got to see what a good salesperson she was. The woman came to the counter to try a blush and left the counter with a blush, an extra makeup brush, and a lip gloss. As soon as the woman was gone, Lissette picked up where she'd left off.

"Now, the thing about Valentino is, he may come in late, leave early, take a long lunch. But when he needs to make the numbers, nobody can sell like he can. And because he's a makeup artist, he can demonstrate, too." She said, lowering her voice a little, "Me, I got plenty of mouth and charm and sex appeal too, but I can't make up anybody else's face as good as I can make up my own. Valentino? He can take an old, beat-up lookin' hen and have her leavin' this counter a swan!"

I laughed.

"I ain't lyin'. You watch him sometime. He's just temperamental. That's his problem. Thinks he's a star and tired of waitin' for his big break. So he's cranky. And downright mean sometimes. That's what happens when you think the world is overlookin' your talent, I suppose. You start getting mean to everybody else you think got talent too. Now, see, that's not me. I know what I can do and what I can't. And I'll get mine. I know it." She flicked her hair, and I wondered what it was she wanted in her life.

Another customer came, and Lissette said a big "Hi" to her like she'd known her for forever. Before she went to her, she said quickly, "The thing about Valentino is, you just don't want to cross him. If he wants something, you let him have it. And then everything works smoothly."

Lissette walked over to the customer. She said so I could hear her, "We were just talking about you. That's our new makeup artist, Carlos. He was saying, 'That woman has the kinda face I would love to work with.' And he doesn't say that often."

I knew my cue. Lissette was trying to get me started, have me get my feet wet. And I was dying to jump in.

"You do have a beautiful face," I said, walking toward the new customer. "And your eyes are gorgeous! Do you have a minute so I could show you a way that you could bring them out more? As a matter of fact, if you started from the very beginning, even before you put on any of your makeup . . ."

chapter 12

When Rosalia came into my room that Sunday morning, I was busy making notes about all the stuff I could say to get people to buy FeatureFace. It wasn't that hard, really, but I wanted to get to the point where I sounded experienced even if I wasn't. I didn't want to sound bored like Valentino sometimes did. No matter what Lissette said, it seemed to me it was obvious he'd rather be anyplace other than where he was. Lissette was right about him being an expert, though. You could tell by watching him completely transform people with the smallest movement of his brush. And he almost always made the right decision about color. He'd barely look at somebody before he started to work on them, and in the beginning I thought, *How can he get it so right that fast?* But Lissette said, "That's his talent, baby. He could paint up an old alligator and have her walk away from this counter and pick up a fine man before she got ten feet away. And I've seen him do it too!"

Then she cackled and tossed her weave. "But when you've been doing it for as long as he has, I guess the thrill is gone!" She looked in the mirror and adjusted one of her false eyelashes. "That's why Miss Lissette's got to hurry up and hook somebody herself. I don't wanna be here as long as Val has, till I get tight and cranky—and we know Val is the queen of tight and cranky!" She cracked herself up again. At least she had a sense of humor about it, I guessed.

The other thing that fascinated me about Valentino was how when he was consulting with a customer and he was really into it, he could sound like he was a surgeon who knew what to cut and how to cut, and could reach for the surgical instrument blindfolded and still pick up the right one.

That's why I was practicing. I had brushes and demo colors, and I rehearsed how I described what I was doing and what product I was using. It was to make sure I made sales and to get to sound like the expert I wanted to be.

"Yo, Carlos." I hated when Rosalia called me by using "Yo," and she knew it. "Why do you have to sound like gangsta girl?" I'd ask her. But I guessed as long as she had Danny for a boyfriend, that's how she was gonna sound. He probably really got off on it.

When I looked up at her, I couldn't move. I couldn't say anything. I could only stare.

"You gotta help me fix this."

"Fix it? I'm not a doctor. Whadya mean 'fix it'? Are you crazy?"

"Why you getting so loud, Carlos? It's not what you think."

"Yeah, right. Your eye is all black and blue and yellow, and you're gonna tell me it's not what I think. Don't even start your lie, 'cause I don't wanna hear it. You wanna lie, you should try it on Ma. See if she doesn't call the cops on that pig!" Now I really was yelling, and I didn't care.

But Rosalia was louder. "And I'm telling you, you're wrong! You think you know everything, but you're wrong!"

I couldn't believe she thought I was that stupid, that I would look at her eye and believe for one minute anything but what I did.

"Now, if you would calm down for one second, I will tell you what happened. And, you know what? I don't care after that if you believe me, because if you think I'm that stupid to be with somebody who would give me a friggin' black eye, then . . . then you just have to believe what you wanna."

"Rosalia, you're crazy," I told her. "You can tell me anything you want to, but you're crazy if you think I believe you."

"Look, I'm telling you the truth. It's after my shift. We're all standin' around in the kitchen, goofin' around. I'm actin' like a nut and I'm showing them how I can cook, and I start pretending I can flip things with the skillet. And the freakin' thing is heavy, but I'm tossin' it around, and I throw it up and I'm supposed to catch it, but the corner comes down and hits me right in the eye. And I swear, I thought it knocked me unconscious. I saw stars!" I stared at my sister, trying to figure out if she's that good an actress, 'cause I'd certainly never seen it before. But she seemed to totally believe what she said, and she seemed to think it was funny even. I didn't say anything. I just kept listening and watching what was either a great performance or a very sad one. Or maybe both.

"And then I woke up this morning and I saw it! I totally understand how you could think what you did, and besides, you don't like Danny anyway—"

"No," I cut her off, "it's not about me liking Danny or not." What I really wanted to say was, "It's about me knowing that Danny's not above giving you a black eye. He's already attacked me."

But I didn't say it. Him hitting me doesn't even compare with him giving Rosalia a black eye. But I did wish I could let her know that I had proof he was capable of being violent for no reason except that the person was there in front of him.

"Rosalia, don't tell me anything else, please. I don't wanna know about the skillet and how you went to sleep with your eye all swollen and you're surprised it turned black and blue. You tell that to somebody else, like Ma. Has Ma seen it?"

"No, she hasn't seen it. Which is why I'm asking you to fix it, put some makeup on it so no one can see it."

"*You* put some makeup on it, Rosalia! You have your own makeup. Why am I gonna help you cover it up?"

"Because she's gonna think the same thing you do, except she'll go crazy and she'll probably call the police on Danny. Like he needs that. Miguel just let him come back to work after he thought he stole from the cash register."

"And you're sure he didn't?"

"Yes, I am! He didn't steal and he didn't hit me, Carlos. I wouldn't lie to you."

Yes, you would, I thought. *And you just did.* "I hope you know that if he hit you once, he'll hit you again. You want two black eyes? Besides not being that attractive, it's not such a healthy thing to keep getting hit in the eye, Rosalia. Why don't you think about that?"

"I'm not gonna tell you again, he did not hit me. Now, are you gonna help me or not?"

I thought for a minute. *Why wouldn't I help her? She's my sister. It's the least I can do. But it's also telling her I'll do it again. And I won't.*

"I'm sorry, Ro. I can't. You wanna cover it up, you figure out how. But I'm not gonna pretend I believe you, and I'm not gonna help you cover it up."

Rosalia stared at me. I couldn't even look back at her, because I couldn't stand staring at her eye. I kept thinking that Danny attacked two people in my family—me *and* my sister—and what was I doing about it? How big a coward was I?

Pretty big, I guess. I left before Ma came home. I didn't want to know if she'd be able to tell what had happened, but I didn't see how she could miss it. And I knew the skillet story would be pure bull to her. God only knew what would happen if Ma saw Rosalia in the same shape she was in when I left.

I was so upset, I called Angie and told her to meet me for pancakes. I eat pancakes when I'm upset. Pancakes with butter. And sausage and bacon. And syrup. Lots of syrup.

chapter 13

I want to be perfectly honest about this, even if it's a little humiliating. Angie is the only one who really knows, and she's sworn to secrecy. For whatever that's worth.

Our code for it is "vegan," which we thought was hysterically funny when we first made it up. I'm a "vegan." What that really means is that I'm a virgin. I've never had a relationship, never had . . . like I said, I'm a "vegan." I've had crushes on people, lots of them. Usually they're guys in magazines or on television. Sometimes just somebody I've passed on the street.

But Gleason Kraft was the first guy to make me think seriously about how anybody who wants to get married should be able to. At first I was only daydreaming about going to Gleason's photography opening. But then I started to think about those articles in decorating magazines I'd seen, where Barry and Sid live in a town house in SoHo and Barry has a photography studio on the third floor. And Sid believes that no matter how busy he is with doing makeup for movies and television, it's important to be at home when the kids come home from school.

The reality was, we said hi to each other in the halls at

school, and when I got up the courage, I yelled out pitiful things like "Can't wait for the opening" and "I guess you must be getting nervous 'cause it's getting so close." But Gleason never said more than "Yeah" and "Naw, I'm okay." I was beginning to think he'd changed his mind. Maybe he *had* started to pick up on how I felt. Maybe he'd heard it in my voice when I asked him those asinine questions and he thought he'd just avoid saying anything to me about the opening again until it had passed. Then he'd make up a lie about why he'd never given me the details.

"You're insane," Angie told me. "True," she said, and laughed, "it is pretty obvious you got the horns for the guy, but I don't think he has a clue."

"Why? Because he'd never think that way about *me*? Or because he isn't gay and he wouldn't think that way about any guy?"

"I hate to tell ya," Angie said, "but I don't think he is. I think with Gleason it's all about the music. Just like with you it's all about the makeup."

"But that's the point," I told her. "It *used* to be all about the makeup. Now it's about the makeup *and* the guy."

Just when I was feeling my most hopeless, I'd laugh. "Well, I guess I better call *Homo House and Gardens* and tell them the article on us is canceled. So much for the freakin' June issue." Then I'd say, "But I'm not giving up. It ain't my naytcha!"

And Angie agreed, "No, hon, givin' up seriously ain't your naytcha!"

Of course, what even Angie didn't know was that I'd found this website online where you could order pretty inexpensive gold chains with charms or medallions or someone's initials. I was looking for an *A* for her birthday, because she'd lost one and she wanted another one. It wasn't exactly my kind of gift, but the price was definitely right. After Gleason told me about his opening, I was looking on the same site to see if there was something I could get him as a present, and I found this tiny, old-fashioned-looking camera that you could put on a chain. It was black, which was perfect for him, and I wasn't sure he'd ever wear it, but I thought it deserved votes for originality, if nothing else. In other words, I thought it was *beyond fabulous*. So I ordered it.

It came in a couple of days, and I'd been putting off showing it to Angie. I carried it around in my bag, trying to figure out if I'd ever get a chance to give it to him.

After the last conversation when I told Angie I wasn't giving up, I waited until she was gone, pulled out the little black camera on the gold chain, and thought how great it was. *I gotta take the chance. Even if he never wears it, I bet he'd keep it and take it out every once in a while and think of me. Like I said, I gotta take the chance.*

Chapter 14

When I got back home, Rosalia wasn't there. Ma was, and she couldn't wait to start in on me.

"Did you see your sister?"

"Whadya mean?" I hedged.

Ma was watching an old movie on television, or at least she had it on. She had a mug of coffee in her lap.

"Don't give me a hard time about this," she said. "It's hard enough as it is. Did you see her or didn't you?"

"Yes," I sighed. "I saw her."

"And you saw her eye?"

"Yeah." I still wasn't going to volunteer anything. I wanted to know exactly what her take on it was before I gave her any information I had.

"What did she tell you about it?" Ma was studying me closely.

"She said she was fooling around with a skillet at work and—"

"So she told you that same lie," Ma barked. "You didn't believe it, did you?"

I sat on the couch. "What do you want me to say, Ma? It was a weird story, but she swore up and down she didn't get hit or anything, so what could I say?" I was whining because I was so frustrated, having to lie about what I really felt and what I knew from my own experience.

"I will tell you what I told her. If she asks you if you think I'm serious, you tell her I am. I don't believe that stupid story about a frying pan. I don't believe it for a minute. But this is what I'm serious about, Carlos. If I find out that bastard Danny has put his hands on her, if I find out that he's hurt her, I will kill him myself." She hadn't even raised her voice, but I knew she meant every word she was saying. And what I was thinking was, *But it should be you, Carlos. It should be you defending your sister. Even if you didn't defend yourself.*

About an hour later Ma got a call from Larry Carridi. Larry was Dominic's brother. Thank God for the Carridi brothers. They believed in family. When Dominic called his brother Larry at the Quick Clean & Press uptown location, Larry said that he could use somebody uptown probably but only part-time. And maybe—"but he ain't promising nothing," Dominic told Ma—there might be a full-time position opening up in a while.

At first Ma wasn't gonna take it. She said, "What kind of money am I gonna make part-time? Nobody in this house eats part-time. The rent sure as hell ain't part-time. No, it's crazy. I'm gonna say no."

But not even twenty minutes later, she changed her mind. "I'm gonna take it."

"Take what?" I asked, because when Ma sounds definite, she *is* definite. So it never occurred to me she was still talking about the Quik Clean & Press thing.

"The part-time job. Even though he says he's not promising

anything, if I get in there and show him I can run his place just like I ran his brother's, I know he'll hire me full-time."

"It's kind of a big chance, Ma, don't you think?" I asked her. But I could tell by the look she was giving me that I was supposed to say, "You're absolutely right. He's got to hire you full-time. How could he possibly not?" So I added really quickly, "I bet he's begging you before you know it!" Ma nodded her head like finally we were doing the same math.

chapter 15

O hmygod, she's baaack!" Lissette was beside herself. She looked like one of those little hula dolls you see in the back windows of cars, shaking and spinning with this ridiculous grin on her face.

"Let's face it," as Michael Kors would say, "stars don't dress like they used to." When Shirlena Day came strutting up to the counter, she could have been a lot of stunning black women in New York, except that she had almost no hair at all, when a lot of girls, like Lissette, were trying to give you *so much hair*. Plus, in every picture I'd ever seen of her, she almost always wore her red *SFN* (*Smokin' Friday Nights*) baseball cap backward, even if she was in an Armani evening gown. (I'm thinkin' that show must have made her a whole lotta money!)

The first Saturday I saw her, she had on high-top Keds and skin-tight jeans with huge rips in the knees, and a huge mustard yellow sweater that mysteriously hung very low in the front but sat up in the back, so you couldn't miss that Ms. Day had a seriously gorgeous bootay. Tight and round and perched, honey, perched!

Like I said, Lissette was going ballistic. She tried to calm herself as Shirlena got closer, but she lost the battle. She started stuttering and stammering like her brain cells were leaking out of her ears. "Oh, MMMMisssDaaay!" she said in this high-pitched squeak.

I might have been embarrassed for her, but it was the day I'd hoped would come. Lissette had told me that Shirlena came in occasionally, and I definitely had been praying for the occasion to get here.

"How are you?" I called to her before she could even get right up to the counter. I guess I made it sound like we knew each other, and that's exactly what I was going for without being rude.

Of course, this is where my manager, the lovely Valentino, would have shoved me to the background so that he alone was standing in front of Shirlena, but because he'd called in with some Valentino crap about waiting for a lock-smith (spelled *h-a-n-g-o-v-e-r*), I got Shirlena all to myself.

"Hey there!" she called back. The sunglasses were already off and she was giving me a HUGE SHIRLENA DAY SMILE.

"I'm Carlos!" I pretty much shouted. I didn't mean for it to be so loud, but I certainly *was* trying for memorable. "Carlos Duarte!" My mouth practically hurt from the grin I was giving her. "At the risk of sounding scarily cheesy, I gotta tell you how much I love . . . that ring!" There! I got her. She sooooo expected me to say what everyone else says that she probably would have bet money on how that sentence would end. I could see the surprise on her face. She held out her right hand and glanced at the roped pearls on her finger. "Me too!" she laughed. "I'm so glad I gave it to myself!"

Lissette was behind me like a big shadow in a weave and

too much perfume. Before she could start in and mess up the moment, I told Shirlena, "Maybe I shouldn't be saying this as a makeup artist, but your skin looks incredible without any." The part about her not having any makeup on was true. The "incredible" part wasn't. I could tell she had oily skin, which I knew must be a problem, because she had to wear so much makeup on TV. And there were teeny bumps on her forehead and chin—fine, though, like a baby rash. They were barely noticeable, but I could see them.

"Actually, that's why I'm here," she said. "Whatever they're using at the studio is making me break out, and I hate it. See." She pointed to her forehead. "And this," she said as she pointed to her chin. I leaned in closer to her as though that was the only way I could see the rash. "Yesssss," I said, sounding like I was looking through a microscope. "It's very subtle, but I see them all right."

"I had a little fit at the studio," Shirlena whispered. "I don't want to be a pain about it, but it's *my* skin, not the makeup artist's! And I keep telling him, and he can't seem to figure out anything to do about it. That other guy who works here, uh, Valentine—"

"Valentino," Lissette piped up. "He's not here right now, but he should be here later today, I guess."

"He's been so good at telling me what to use, I thought maybe he could help with this."

"We don't actually know when Valentino is coming in today," I said as carefully as I could, "but I'd be happy to help you if I can."

Just at that moment another customer came rushing up to the counter. Thank God, Lissette turned her attention toward her and left Shirlena and me alone.

"Is it for all your makeup on the show, or is it just for your Michelle O character?"

But the woman with Lissette apparently wasn't interested in FeatureFace at all. She'd really come over for Shirlena's autograph. Shirlena turned from our conversation and quickly signed the scrap of paper the woman had stuck in her face. Then the woman said, "Oh, could you please sign one for my next-door neighbor, too? She'll kill me when I tell her I got an autograph and didn't get one for her, too. She watches SFN even more than I do."

I could tell Shirlena was a little frustrated. So I said, "I'm sorry. Ms. Day and I are having a consultation." The woman was still fumbling in her bag. Shirlena smiled at me, but she purred, "Oh, no. I don't mind signing one more."

The woman looked up and glared at me. She said to Shirlena, "Never mind. I can't find anything for you to sign. I was gonna ask *him*, but—" And she gave me a dirty look. I saw Lissette start to look under the counter for a piece of paper, but I caught her eyes and sent her a *Don't you dare!* message.

"Thanks anyway, Shirlena," the woman said, as if they were old friends.

And Shirlena once again turned on the Shirlena brights. "Maybe next time!"

When the woman had gone, Shirlena said to me, "Honey, you are gooood!"

And I was thrilled. "What I'm thinking," I told her, "is that if we can duplicate what your makeup artist is using on the show, we have a line that is completely hypoallergenic, so he or she—your makeup artist—should be able to use it on you without any reaction!"

"See! Great minds think alike!" And it was definitely not the Shirlena-smiles-for-the-fans smile she was giving me. "I wasn't sure it could be done, but I thought it was worth a try. Anything to get rid of these bumps. They're driving me crazy! Christian, my makeup artist on *SFN*, is really talented, but a little lazy and a little temperamental. Not a good combination. I keep saying, 'We have to do something about this, Christian!' and he keeps saying yes, and every week I break out all over again."

"Well, you know it's going to take some experimenting. What we'd have to do is get everything Christian uses now and see if we can replace it with a FeatureFace product. I'm sure it can be done, but . . ." I stopped and took a breath. I couldn't believe what I was about to say. "I wish there was some way I could get my hands on whatever it is Christian uses. Then I could just work out the replacements myself and he wouldn't have to do it."

"God, you're such a doll!" Shirlena chirped. "Like I told you, he's a little on the lazy side, so maybe I could take your card and give it to him. And he could get in touch with you."

"Absolutely! That would be *beyond excellent!*" Shirlena looked at me as if she thought my enthusiasm was a little overboard, but I didn't care. There was no way she could know how excited I was for this chance.

"Why don't you give me one of your cards?" she asked me again.

"Oh! Yes. My card." I didn't have any card. Lissette, who hadn't missed a second, handed me a FeatureFace card.

"I'm getting a new batch printed up, but is this all right for now?" I asked Shirlena, taking the card from Lissette and handing it to her.

"Sure," Shirlena chuckled. "You got your number on here?"

"I will have," I said, feeling ridiculous, "in just a second!" I grabbed a pen and scribbled my name and cell number on the card. I was careful to spell my name Carrlos on the card. "I really want to help you with this, and I'm sure I can!" I was gushing.

Shirlena was gathering her bag and getting ready to go just as another group of girls was headed for her. "I'm going to give Christian your card for sure. He should call you this week. I don't want to do one more show wearing that stuff he already has. So, thanks, honey!" She was putting on her dark glasses and sending off signals to the approaching army that she was in a hurry.

"Don't worry," I called to her. "I know I can fix every-thing!" It sounded like I was willing to move in, scrub her floors, and handle her bills and all of her legal matters. I was only hoping it didn't sound pathetic and desperate. 'Cause what I felt was the opposite. If she only gave me a chance, or if Christian did, I knew I could come through for her. "Make sure he calls me!" I shouted as she was moving through the store with the girls shoving paper at her.

"Valentino is gonna kill you!" Lissette squealed.

"Why?" I answered innocently. "All I did was take care of the customer. Isn't that why he hired me?" Shirlena was not quite out of sight. I yelled across the store floor in her direction, "Don't forget it's Carrlos with two r's!"

I turned back to Lissette. "Like I said. Just taking care of the customer!"

Chapter 16

Sometimes there are things in life you want really badly, but they're not in the plan, so you can want them till it rains Hershey's kisses, and it's not gonna happen. This is something I heard my ma say, and I was trying really hard to think it didn't apply to me going to Gleason's show.

I was beginning to wonder why he ever said he'd invite me to it. Maybe he meant it when he said it, and then changed his mind because he saw how geeked-out I got about it. Or his friends saw him speak to me and gave him crap. I couldn't tell. All I knew was that days had gone by and it seemed like it was some kind of delusion.

Until the afternoon when I was on my way out of school and I got a call from him and I almost lost control of my bladder. He had my number from when he took my model makeup pictures, but I'd always been the one to get in touch with him.

"Yes," I answered, half expecting it would be somebody playing a cruel joke.

"Hey, it's Gleason." He sounded shy, but then he almost always sounded shy. "I wanted to know if you would look at something for me."

"Yeah . . . sure." Whatever it was, wherever it was, no matter what time it was, the answer would have been the same.

"Could you, uh, meet me at my locker? It's on the first floor."

"I remember." I knew very well where his locker was. I even knew what number it was—728. The number was scratched, so you might not have been able to tell it was a seven except that it was between 727 and 729. It was next to the biology lab and I was halfway down the stairs by the time I got off my cell.

Gleason was standing next to his open locker. I slowed down and tried not to look as though I had run like a well-trained dog when he called.

"Hey," I said, and it sounded about as casual as if I'd said, "I came as soon as I could get down the stairs. I've been waiting for a call, a letter, an e-mail, anything!"

"Hey," Gleason said. "I wanted to show you something. Get your opinion."

I was thinking, *Anything! Show me anything!*

Gleason took out what looked like pieces of paper wrapped in plastic. "I was thinking maybe you could tell me what would be the best mat to use for my photographs."

"Oh!" I was really surprised. I didn't know anything about mats. I wasn't sure I knew what they were.

Gleason pulled the pieces of paper out of the wrapping. "These are just the samples, of course. They can be wider or narrower or pretty much any color I want." I understood then that they were paper frames for the photographs. "I was thinking about black, 'cause I think that would be more dramatic. But maybe that's cheesy."

"What's cheesy about being dramatic?" I said, maybe a little too loudly. "Your photos are dramatic."

Gleason laughed. "Is that a good thing?"

"You betta believe it's a good thing!" I told him. "I wouldn't do gold or silver. But black is perfect."

"Do you want to see the other samples? I've got gray and white and off-white."

"You can show 'em to me if you want, but I'm pretty sure we made the right decision." Did I love saying "we" or what?

Gleason pulled out the other samples, and I examined them carefully. I wanted to make sure he understood how seriously I took him asking me for my opinion. "Do you have any of the photographs with you, so I could make sure?"

"I have one of them," he said. He pulled a small portfolio out of his locker. "I'm still trying to decide how big I should have them printed."

"Are you kidding?" I said. "For your first show? Go as big as you can!"

Gleason smiled. "The bigger they are, the more expensive."

"Oh," I said, coming back down to earth. I'd immediately started to see the billboard-size photos I'd already imagined. "Well, as big as you can afford, then."

"You think they're that good for me to have them printed big?"

He pulled out of his portfolio a print that he'd taken of Rosalia. It was larger already than the one he had given me to take to Macy's. Immediately my eyes went to my sister's eyes. I remembered her saying when I was making them up, "The good thing about you is that you're gentle,

Carlos. Nobody will complain that you're being too rough. I couldn't have anybody who was too rough doing anything to my eyes."

Now when I was looking into my sister's eyes in Gleason's photograph, I thought that somebody had been more than rough with her. Somebody had been an animal.

"I don't know if they're good enough to have them printed bigger than this," Gleason said quietly.

"I think they're great," I told him. "Really. Great."

"Cool." Gleason the rocker nodded. "Cool." He started to wrap up the mat samples.

I took a breath. "I wasn't sure you still wanted me to come to the show," I told him.

"Why not?" he asked, looking surprised.

"It's been a while since you first told me about it. I don't even know when it is." I was trying not to sound too anxious.

"This weekend," Gleason said casually. "Friday night." He added, "You're still coming, right?"

Again I worked hard on sounding as casual as possible. "Sure. Especially since now I've been the adviser to the photographer on what mats to choose. That's pretty important, isn't it?" Not that I was trying to make it crystal clear how much he needed me in his life for multiple reasons, or anything like that.

"Absolutely." Gleason smiled at me, and I swear the fluorescents in our school's ugly hallway had a pinkish lavender glow.

"So how could I not be there?" I said to him, and gave him the same look I give the photographers in my daydream interviews. And I held it for a second so he'd remember it.

Then I got my inspiration. I dug into my bag and found

the little camera that I'd ordered for him online. I held it out, laughing, although inside I was suddenly a twitching clump of nerves.

"I was going to give this to you at the opening," I said in this voice that wasn't quite mine, "but maybe it will inspire you while you're trying to arrange everything."

What made it truly horrifying was that he stood there without moving or saying anything for what seemed like ten minutes. He was frozen, looking down at the little plastic bag with the camera on a chain in it like I was handing him a plastic bag of drugs in the middle of our school hallway.

When he finally snapped out of it, I was ready to take it back and run. "Thanks, man," he said. "Really, thanks." He reached out and patted me lamely on the shoulder. I, of course, had envisioned a big, long bear hug.

Thank God I'm good at pulling it together fast. "Hope everything works out with the mats," I told him and I was already moving away.

"Carlos!" he called, and I stopped. When I turned around, I was prepared for anything. He might give me back the camera, he might tell me not to come to the opening, anything.

"I'm glad you're coming to the opening. And you shouldn't have doubted me, man. How could I show those pictures and not have you there?"

That was enough to calm my nerves and put a grin on my face. I started hearing "You shouldn't have doubted me, man" like it was the chorus of a song that filled my whole body and wouldn't stop.

chapter 17

Now that I was sure I was going to Gleason's opening, I decided to ask Soraya to go with me as my date. We hadn't spoken since I returned the ruined Stella McCartneys, except when I went to Tokyo Jo's to give her twenty dollars as a payment installment and she refused it. "I don't mean to be rude, Carlos, but twenty dollars on a pair of three-hundred-dollar boots? You're kidding, right?" I told her I was serious. It was just that my ma had just been laid off and I needed to give her more money for rent and stuff around the house.

Soraya said, "Then you should forget about trying to buy these boots, because by the time you finish paying for them, I won't even be working here. You may not even know how to get in touch with me, and I certainly won't be accepting payments for boots that were destroyed back when I had a part-time job."

I knew that she was pissed, and I was pretty sure she was determined to hold a grudge, but I was just as determined to get my friend back. No, there was no excuse for me wearing the boots outside of Macy's when I swore up and down that I wouldn't. But up until then, Soraya and I had been really close, and if at all possible, I wasn't going to let our relationship go down the toilet, even over a pair of designer boots.

The store was crowded when I got there, but Soraya saw me right away. The store is tiny, so she sees everyone when they first come in. Plus, it's so crowded that she has to watch for shoplifters—or, as we used to joke, shoplifters with not just skills but good taste.

Soraya saw me, but she didn't even speak to me at first. She was standing up on her platform above the sales floor, where the cash register was. The other girl who works with her, Justine, was standing on the main floor. She was there mostly to rehang clothes that people either dropped over the racks or left on the floor of the dressing room after they'd realized they couldn't fit into a size four.

"Hi, Carlos," Justine called out to me nervously. She knew what had happened between me and Soraya, but she was still hoping for the best, I guess, knowing how close we'd been.

"Hi, hon," I called back. Then I stood near the platform where Soraya towered above me, ignoring me as she rang up customers' sales. When there was a slight break, I took the opportunity to say meekly, "Do you think you have a few minutes? I really want to ask you something."

Soraya looked down at me from her perch next to the cash register. She was loving looking down at me too. Her whole body was saying so. "You can see I'm busy, Carlos. What is it that you want?"

I just had to eat the attitude, swallow it whole, and know that it would be worth it in the end. "You remember Gleason Kraft, the kid who took my model pictures?" It all of a sudden occurred to me that maybe it wasn't the smartest idea to bring up the model pictures at all, but I was only doing it to make her remember who Gleason was.

"Yeah, I remember," Soraya said, and I knew I had definitely started to pick at an unhealed wound.

"A gallery is showing his photography and he invited me to the opening—"

"And what, Carlos? *What*?" She was so loud, people were turning around to stare at us. I am not one to be embarrassed in public, not by my friends, at least. My ma is the only one allowed to do that, and she takes full advantage of the privilege often enough. But I pushed on. I was there for a cause. I was on a sacred mission.

"And I'm here to ask you if you would please go with me."

It was obvious that Miss Soraya-Anna-Wintour-Girl was surprised. But she recovered quickly.

"You have nerve, Carlos, colossal nerve."

"I know, girl. So do you. Now, will you go with me?" I was trying to sound flip, like *Get over it, girl, so we can get back to being friends.*

Soraya stepped down off the platform. "Carlos, you really don't get it, do you? You are so self-centered, so determined to get what you want when you want it, that you will say anything, do anything, and when you lie and the lie backfires, you want people to forget it happened. Because . . . because why? Because the whole world should do whatever you want 'cause you won't grow up and take responsibility for what you do and say?"

By now people were *pretending* to shop, but I could tell they were listening to see what happened next.

"I've already said I was sorry, Soraya. And I am. I offered to pay for the boots, and you said no."

"You offered me twenty dollars for a pair of three-hundred-dollar boots, Carlos!"

"It was a payment. It was all I had."

"Well, you know what? Now my boss is making *me* pay for them, so I *will* take your measly twenty dollars, and you can keep giving me money for as long as it takes until you've paid for the boots you brought back ruined!"

I was shocked. I thought she might say no to going to the opening, but I wasn't prepared for all this drama. Soraya's eyes, hands, neck, and hips were all going in different directions at the same time. I reached into my bag for my wallet.

"If that's the first payment you're reaching for, it better be good. You better try for *more* than twenty!"

I couldn't believe her. "Soraya, why are you being like this? Is this really the end of our friendship because I made a mistake?"

"Don't give me that, Carlos. If it's the end of our friendship, it's because you said you could be trusted and you can't. Who needs a friend you can't trust? Not me!"

I realized I had three dollars in my wallet. It was definitely not the time to offer Soraya three dollars. It was also clear that some people around me were waiting to see what I was going to come up with. I quickly tucked the wallet back into my bag.

"I'll start my payments this week. I just don't have enough on me right now."

"I'll believe it when I see it, Carlos!" Soraya gave me one last horrible look, then got back on her platform.

I shook my head and sighed like I thought she was making some ridiculous, irrational mistake, but it was to save face in front of the customers. I knew she had a right to be furious with me. Slinging my bag up onto my shoulder, I mumbled good-bye to Justine, who was looking at me sadly as if she'd just watched Soraya slice off my fingers one at a time.

When I got outside, I walked until I was past the store windows, where people could see me. Then I stopped. *What a fool, Carlos*, I said to myself. *All because of those ridiculous boots. It's not as though you couldn't have done the same job on Rosalia's makeup without wearing shoes that weren't even yours. Do you really think they cared that you had on those stupid boots?* Oh, well. It was done now. Over. The only thing I could hope was that by the time I'd finished making my payments to Soraya, she'd decide to forgive me. If not, lesson learned. The next time I'd be wearing Stella McCartney boots, they'd be ones I owned.

Just when I thought the day couldn't get uglier, I was at the corner when I saw one of the boys from Burrito Take-Out Village coming toward me. Not the one who'd actually ruined the boots. And not Danny. It was the third thug. He might even have passed me without looking at me. He didn't seem to see me. But I stared at him, and he looked at me just as I passed him. We both turned around. I could tell he definitely recognized me then, because of the big sneer. I gave him the dirtiest look I could. I made my eyes say, *Yeah, it's me. Now you come back here and try to do something to me again.*

But he didn't even sneer for that long. The sneer turned

into a snicker, which turned into a laugh. I stopped. I was ready to kill him. I wished they were all there, especially Danny. Whatever was going to happen to me would just have to happen. I wished they were all there right this minute so I could do what I should have done on the steps of the subway station.

But it didn't happen. Burrito Guy gave me this look like I was a toddler he'd knocked over and he thought it was a joke to see me bounce off the pavement. And I mouthed, "Screw you," totally ready for him to come at me. But he laughed some more and turned around and walked away. I watched him till he turned the corner. Then I said "Pig" and kept going.

chapter **18**

Gleason Kraft's opening was in a gallery on Mercer Street in SoHo. I knew Mercer Street really well because that's where the Marc Jacobs store was. I could never afford to buy anything there, but me and Angie had been lots of times to stare at the clothes, and so had me and Soraya.

The gallery was called La Menagerie. I thought I knew what that meant, except I thought it was a weird name for a gallery. When I looked up "menagerie" in the dictionary, it was even more confusing. There was one definition that said "wild animal exhibition," which is what I thought a menagerie was, and another that said "diverse, exotic, or unusual group of people or things." I supposed that was the definition whoever owned the gallery was thinking of when they named it. Did that mean that the gallery owner thought that Gleason's photographs were exotic or unusual? I kind of thought Gleason was. Because he was a rocker and a photographer and he was serious and intelligent and talented and gorgeous. And did that make him exotic or unusual? Well, when I thought of most of the other guys in school, he definitely was.

The opening was from six to eleven on Friday night.

From the time I got home from school on Friday, I started getting ready. I went to a nail salon near our apartment and got a manicure. I'd always wanted to get manicures anyway, and after I got hired by FeatureFace, I told myself it was a professional necessity. I thought about how Gleason sometimes wore nail polish, but it was black and he could get away with it because of the rocker thing. Except I'm sure some people still made comments, but that's the way it was in our school. You could get away with anything. You just had to do it with confidence or they could make your life miserable, simply because a lot of them didn't *have* lives.

While the woman was doing one hand, I called Angie. "I know what you said about giving Gleason the camera charm, but I still think I shouldn't show up to the opening emptyhanded!"

When I told Angie about the camera charm, we'd almost gotten into a huge argument. She'd insisted I'd gone too far by giving Gleason a present, and I thought it was perfectly harmless and hoped he'd do the same if I had something to celebrate.

So Angie said, "We've already gone through this and almost ruined our friendship. What are you going to get him now, a car?"

"Don't be a creep, Ange. I don't have money for anything, really, but I know I can't just walk in and say hi without anything to give him. It will be humiliating."

Angie sighed. "Okay, Carlos. I'm tired of telling you to be careful with that boy. Do what you want."

"Okay," I said sharply. "Let's meet at the Eighth Street subway and take the train down, like I said." I hung up thinking maybe I was sorry I'd invited her. It was bad enough she made a comment about being Soraya's understudy. Totally unfair. She was always exaggerating things.

I went home, showered, and shampooed. The whole time I was thinking how much I hoped I would get some sign from Gleason at the opening that he liked me as much as I knew he did. My psychology teacher always says, "Showing up is the first move toward achieving your goal," and I was thinking I'd already given him the charm, so showing up at the gallery was really step two, or at least step one plus. If Gleason just took his first step, I'd be more than glad to take steps three, four, and five.

Probably he'd be wearing all black. That was Gleason's signature look. Black and red. I didn't want to compete or, God forbid, upstage him, so I decided on my antique white tuxedo shirt, to let him know what a special occasion I knew this was and also because the tuxedo shirt made me look pretty incredible. I wore my burgundy smoking jacket, almost-skinny black jeans, and these stiletto-toed patent leathers with Cuban heels. I slicked my hair back, and finally I dusted my face ever so slightly with just enough color to make me look what I called "sun-kissed."

Of course when Angie saw me, the first thing she said was, "I'm really surprised you think that's subtle, Carlos. You're a professional makeup artist. You look like you got caught in a blush storm!" Then she laughed hysterically, like she thought she was giving Kathy Griffin something to worry about. She stopped when she saw how beyond unfunny I'd found it.

"I'm sorry, hon," she cooed. "I'm only trying to be a good friend and tell you the truth. I know you're trying to impress the boy, but you don't want to show up looking like RuPaul either, do you? And wouldn't you want me to tell you the truth if that's what I thought?"

"Yeah, Ange. RuPaul, huh? That's definitely not what I was going for. I don't know how I could have miscalculated so badly." I never, ever fix my makeup in public—I think it's tacky when anyone does. But I didn't want to walk into the gallery with the blush storm effect either, so even though I don't usually take makeup or fashion tips from Angie, who was in very large polka dots, I took a little color off just to make sure.

When I went to a flower stand outside a little bodega and bought a dozen roses to give to Gleason, Angie kept her opinions to herself. I'm sure she knew she'd ruin the evening if she said anything at all about it. I got a little card and wrote, "To a great guy who takes great pictures. From one of your biggest admirers." I would have said "absolute biggest," but I was trying to be subtle.

La Menagerie was on the first floor and we could see the smokers out on the sidewalk as we were coming down the block. It was an older crowd, definitely older than we were. There were guys in suits and those New York girls who you couldn't really picture doing any specific job, but they all looked like they bought what the magazines told them to buy. They could have all been extras in any movie about New York City thirtysomethings.

When we got inside, it was pretty crowded, mostly because the gallery was small and winding, like a tunnel with photos on the walls. I wasn't even looking at anybody else's work. I was only looking for Gleason.

Around a corner he was surrounded by rockers that were our age. They weren't kids from school, which didn't surprise me. But to tell you the truth, I didn't really see them, either. It was like one of those movies where everything else goes blurry except the person you're looking at, who's in perfect focus.

Just like I'd guessed, Gleason had on all black. He was doing this cowboy thing with a black on black cowboy shirt, complete with one of those string ties—which, to be really honest, I would have found a little corny on anybody else at any other time. But not tonight.

He was talking to a girl with cranberry-colored hair and green eye shadow. It was clear from 180 feet away that Gleason could have been reciting the thirty-six most commonly used prepositions in alphabetical order and she would have been mesmerized. The other kids were looking at the photos and calling out things like, "Awesome" and "Sooo cool!" I stopped in my tracks, causing Angie to almost knock me over. Which, of course, immediately started her giggling.

But I kept staring at Gleason and the girl with cranberry hair. Now she was hugging him as though she was hanging from a tall building with no net under her. I couldn't see Gleason's face, but his arms were around her and he wasn't letting go. What if I was totally deluded? What if I didn't stand an ice cube's chance in a pot of Lipton that Gleason and me . . .

Oh, well. Too late now. My heart was crumbling around the edges, but I kept walking toward them. At least I looked good, I thought.

As I got closer, Cranberryhead happened to turn her

body so that Gleason could see me over her shoulder. It was unmistakable. His eyes brightened and he grinned at me. "Heeeeey!"

Cranberryhead immediately pulled away from him, but she wasn't letting go. Gleason had to give himself a little tug before he was free.

"You showed, man!" *Man?*

But he reached for me. It seemed to be in slow motion. I felt his arms go around me, and I was trying to stay on my feet. He actually stepped on my right foot, but I didn't dare move it or try to get my foot out from under his. I closed my eyes and could feel how skinny he was. I held on to his back and put my face against his hair. His shoulder was under my chin. *Can he feel me shaking? Does he think I'm scared or on drugs?* Either way, I didn't let go, even though I knew all the roses were probably mashed together like peanut butter cups between us. In the background, there was music playing. I don't know what the actual song was, but, of course, what I heard was "Here Comes the Bride." And I went for it. I kissed him. Yeah, on the cheek, but I kissed him. And I was glad I did it. I had no idea what Gleason thought about it, but he didn't throw me across the room, so I considered that a plus.

Then he said to Cranberryhead, "Gabs, this is Carlos. If it wasn't for him, there wouldn't be any model pictures."

"Yes. You've said that," Cranberryhead told him flatly.

But Gleason continued, grinning. "You were right, Carlos! They look so cool really big. And people keep asking me who the girls are and whether they're models or actresses or both."

I looked up at the photo of Rosalia smiling out at the

room. *I have to bring her here to see herself this way*, I thought. How different she looked from the Rosalia I saw stuck behind that counter asking people if they wanted chips and salsa with their burritos. There was nothing wrong with what she did, I just wanted her to understand she could do so much more.

"All the photos look great," I told him. "Congratulations!" And I held the roses up. For an instant it felt like the moment when I'd held up the plastic bag with the charm in it.

He said "Whooaa" quietly and took them. "Thanks." Gleason didn't look at me. Instead he took a quick look in Cranberryhead's direction. Then he said, "And thanks for the advice about the mats. Black was definitely the way to go."

Not the reaction to the roses I wanted, but I was sure it was because he was shy and hadn't expected them. I just had to get used to the idea that Gleason wasn't someone who was comfortable accepting presents. I was still happy I gave them to him. I thought, *He needs me. He's going to be famous and he needs me. This is only the first show. There'll be hundreds, and I'll have to be there for him. To help him with the mats. To help him figure out what to wear. And to tell the magazines, "Yeah, it's hard with my own career being so successful, but we always find time to be there for each other."*

Cranberryhead was suddenly looking very confused and unhappy. "Are you going to stand here all night in front of your photographs? The place isn't that big. It's not as though people can't find them. We should go to the bar and have a glass of wine."

"You two wanna go have a glass of wine with me and Gabs? You look really good, by the way," Gleason said to Angie.

I could tell by the look on Cranberryhead's face that that's not what she had in mind.

"You guys go ahead. I wanna stay here and look at these for a while," I said, gesturing toward the photos. Gleason gave me what I thought was a pretty weak smile as Cranberryhead dragged him away still holding on to the roses.

I pointed toward the two of them moving toward the bar, Gabs with her arm inside Gleason's and her head practically on his shoulder. "What kinda person wants to be called Gabs?"

"Oh, come on," Angie told me. "At least he seems happy that you're here."

"You think so? It didn't stop him from going off with *Gabs*. She's clinging to him like a leech in heels."

Angie laughed. "Why are you so evil? He has the roses, doesn't he?"

"I'm not evil at all. Don't you think it's about time I . . ."

"What? Actually had a relationship?" As close as we were, Angie and me had never talked directly about me having a relationship with anybody. Even though I had known her through at least five of her boyfriends, whether they were for two months or six, I'd never had any to talk about. I called people my boyfriends to get a laugh, as though she took for granted how far from the truth it was. Even my ma said, "I thought in high school, kids had some kinda girlfriends or boyfriends or somethin', but you don't ever bring anyone in here but Angie. You're not going out with *her*, are ya?" I said, "You know I'm not," and she said, "That's exactly what I mean."

I wanted somebody I could daydream about living with,

having the cute puppy with, the apartment, the house in the country, and the rings that had our secret messages engraved on the inside of the band.

And yes, I had started to think about whether Gleason would like a girl puppy or a boy puppy and whether he'd like a summer beach house or one in the country. I even thought of how he'd need enough space to practice his music *and* a photography studio, so I'd better get rich and successful fast so we could start living happily ever after sooner rather than later. Dumb, huh? Well, to me it was *beyond romantic*. It was the only way I wanted to live my life.

Me and Angie stood in front of Gleason's photographs. I was going on and on about how, "I really do think we're a good couple, don't you? We look good together, we're both artistic, and I bet he'd be really proud of me if he knew how famous I was going to be and that we'll be celebrities together."

But it was Angie who finally brought me thudding back to earth with, "He doesn't seem to be in any hurry to come back here. Where do you think him and Gabs disappeared to?"

"The bar?" I said weakly. Of course I was disappointed that he hadn't come back with maybe even a drink of wine or champagne as thanks for helping him make his first show a success.

"Then, I think we should go to the bar," Angie said firmly. "We've been standing here for years, and I'm bored. The pictures are great, but there are other people in this show and there are lots of cute guys in this gallery. So can we please move to the bar?"

We left Gleason's photographs and headed into the

main room, where most of the people were. The music was louder there, and it was more full than it had been when we'd first come in. You couldn't really see who was at the bar from where we were standing, but it took me about two and a half seconds to look through the crowd and spot Gleason and *Gabs*. They had their backs to us, and Cranberryhead had her arm around Gleason's waist. The worst part of the picture was that Gabs was holding the roses I'd given to Gleason, and it couldn't have been because they were too heavy for him to carry.

Angie saw the same thing I did. She said, "What do you want to do?"

"Leave," I said.

Angie was quiet for a moment. Then she said something only Angie could have come up with. "Maybe he's allergic. And he didn't want to say anything because he didn't want to hurt your feelings."

"Excellent try, Ange. Can we go now, please?"

But I guess I didn't decide to leave fast enough, because that's when I looked over and saw Gleason *really* kissing Gabs.

"Damn," I whispered, and looked away.

"Oh, no," Angie said quietly. "Ohmygod."

We stood there for a minute in silence before she said, "Carlos, I'm sorry."

I faked a laugh. "Why? I'm the one who made up the freaking fairy tale. Nobody told *him* I wanted to marry him."

Gabs and Gleason stopped kissing. As though she'd heard her name being called, Gabs looked back to where Angie and me were standing. I gave her a saran wrap smile—like it was being held in place by a thin layer of plastic.

"Are you going to say anything to him?" Angie asked me.

"Yeah," I said dramatically. "Adios."

I walked over to where Gleason and Gabs were, with Angie following me. Gleason lit up as though he was seeing me for the first time that night. "There you are!"

I wasn't about to go off into some dream world again. "Hi. We came to say we're leaving."

"You're kidding. You practically just got here. Aren't you gonna at least have a glass of wine?"

"No, we really have to go," I said, and Angie slipped her arm in mine for support.

"Here, I'll walk you out," Gleason said. "I'll be right back," he told Gabs.

"Good night," I managed to get out to Gleason's girl-friend, or friend or whatever. I glanced down at the roses in her hand and wished I could take them from her and toss them into a garbage can on my way out. Gleason wasn't even pretending that he hadn't given her the flowers I'd brought for him.

When we got to the door, there was a thick knot of people. I turned to him to say good-bye again, but he put his hand on my back and pushed me through until he and Angie and me were all outside the gallery on the sidewalk.

Then suddenly he was hugging me, holding on tight. The minute he touched me, I was confused all over again.

"Just so you know," he said, not letting go of me, "the gallery owner just told me that the best decision I made was to include the shots of the girls." I swear I could feel his breath on my ear. "And all I could think of was that it was because of you, Mr. Genius Guy."

"That's really . . . sweet." I laughed nervously, not understanding at all what was going on.

"I'm serious. You're the best!" Gleason backed away and said to Angie and me, "See ya."

I stared at him, trying to make some sense of the whole thing. It was as though he and I had jumped into our own private movie for twenty seconds, then right back out into reality. I wanted to ask him, "Who are you, anyway?"

Somebody called him. As he was going back inside, the last thing I heard Gleason say was, "Hey, man!" to whoever had called him. He sounded like the rocker guy from school who I occasionally ran into in the hallways.

But he didn't sound at all like the same guy who'd just held me. Maybe they were the same person, maybe they weren't. I'd thought I wanted to leave, but the second Gleason was gone, I missed him.

chapter 19

C arlos?"
          It was a guy's voice, and at first I thought it might be
Gleason. Or maybe I was hoping.

I was in the tub. Taking a bubble bath. I'd put the phone
up on the sink just in case. I didn't want to miss the call.

"Yes, this is Carlos," I answered. What came out next
at the other end sounded like "Christmas New Year," and I
almost hung up.

"I'm sorry, who did you say this is?"

"Christian Newtier." The voice reminded me of
Valentino's. So bored-sounding, as though it was a real
chore to have a telephone conversation. "I *thought* Shirlena
Day said you'd be *expecting* my call."

I jumped to my feet in the tub and ran my hand over my
hair like Christian Newtier on the other end could see it.

"Oh! Christian! Of course! I *was* expecting your call!"

All I could think of was that I didn't know all of the
FeatureFace products' names and I'd sound like a fool if he
asked me for a recommendation. There was dead silence on
the other end.

"Shirlena said she wanted me to replace the makeup you were using with FeatureFace products because of her allergies," I blurted.

"Oh, really? What she told *me* was that you were going to suggest something from your line and then I'd try it to see how I liked it."

There I was standing in the middle of my bathtub, with soap bubbles on my shoulders, feeling stupid and speechless. I hadn't expected him to sound like the Wicked Witch of the West. I may as well have gotten a call from Valentino.

"Whatever I can do to help," I said, trying my best to sound like Glinda.

"Can you send over the hypoallergic makeup you told her about, and I'll see if I can use any of it."

Hypoallergic?

I looked at my phone as if it was him, and I mouthed "Pitiful" at it.

"I'm really sorry, Christian, but I can't send the whole line over because I don't know what you need and—well, maybe I could—I guess I'd have to ask my manager, but wouldn't it be easier if you came in and we could go over what you needed and I could help you figure out—"

"You know what? I have to go out to dinner and I'm late already. Just send over the hypoallergic line tomorrow and I'll take a look at it." And he hung up.

"What a dork!" I said out loud. "Did you ever hear the word 'hypoallergenic'? As if you care! You probably couldn't give a damn if Shirlena's whole head breaks out and blows up! Enjoy your dinner, ya creep!"

Chapter 20

From the minute Christian Newtier hung up on me, I worried about how to get Shirlena the makeup she needed when I didn't know exactly *what* she needed or even how to get it to her. Christian was being such a pain in the butt, he didn't give me an address to have the makeup delivered to. I thought about getting it ready in case he sent a messenger, but there was still the matter of sending him the entire line of makeup when it probably wasn't necessary. Not that Shirlena couldn't afford it, and it would be good business for FeatureFace *and* for me, but I didn't want her to think I was trying to take advantage of her.

By the next morning I'd decided not to say anything to Valentino. If Christian called me back, I'd deal with it then. But I wasn't going to have Valentino take over the situation and come to Shirlena's rescue when the opportunity had come to me.

Of course, Lissette had already told him about Shirlena coming in. I was in Intro to Bio (yuck) when the first call came. My pants started to vibrate, and I slid my phone out to check it. There it was:

Incoming Messages: (1) Valentino

Ugh! Usually I'd be ecstatic, because it meant extra work at the store. But this time I knew it was trouble. I called him back right after class.

"I understand Shirlena came into the store, and you worked with her. Lissette said you made some kind of deal with her—"

"I didn't make any deals, Valentino. She needed help and I tried to help her."

"Shirlena Day is *my* customer. I know everything about what she needs. What was it?"

I didn't want to tell him. I'd had the conversation with her, and she didn't ever say she'd rather be working with Valentino. Why did I have to turn over all my information to him? Because he was my boss, that's why.

"She said she's allergic to the makeup they're using on her for *Smokin' Friday Nights*. I said we had a hypoallergenic line and I'd be happy to work with her makeup guy for the show to see if we could substitute what they're using on her now."

"*You'd* be happy to work with him? That won't happen. I told you, Shirlena is *my* customer. She's bought thousands of dollars of FeatureFace from *me*! So what's supposed to happen next? Is Shirlena going to call you, or is the makeup artist?"

"The makeup artist. And he already did."

"He already did what?"

"Call me."

"He *did*? And when were you going to tell me?" By now he was practically screaming. It was ridiculous. I could imagine everyone around the counter in the store staring.

"I'm sorry, Valentino," I said, not feeling at all sorry.

"The thing is, I still don't know what Shirlena needs. The makeup artist called and he asked for the whole hypoallergenic line to be sent over today—"

"Fine. Where does he want it sent?"

"I don't know."

"What do you mean you don't know? Didn't he give you an address?"

"No, Valentino, he *didn't*." I soooo didn't want to be having this conversation with him.

"Give me his number. I'll call him back and get the address."

I rolled my eyes. I knew it was only going to get worse. "I don't have his number. Shirlena took my number and gave it to him."

"Are you lying to me?" This took me by surprise, although I suppose it shouldn't have. Actually, if I'd thought about it, I probably could have found Christian's number on my incoming calls, but all I could concentrate on was getting off the phone with him.

"I don't have the number," I repeated quietly.

"How convenient."

I waited for any other snarky comment he could lash out with. I had no choice. Then I realized he'd hung up on me.

At that moment, yes, I did think that the whole thing with Shirlena had been one big joke on me that had exploded in my face. Valentino would fire me, and that would be the end of it. *Beyond tragic.* It sucked.

chapter 21

You're gonna look down your nose at your own sister now?"

That's exactly what my mother accused me of. "Why?" she was shouting. "Because you got a job in Macy's selling makeup on the weekends? That's what makes you so hoity-toity now?"

"No, Ma. Macy's has nothing to do with it." And I knew she was being especially nasty because I'd told her a thousand times I wasn't a salesperson, I was a makeup artist. But now, to make her point about me and Rosalia, she had to belittle my job. "I'm not looking down my nose at Rosalia. I'm only saying that people have choices, and if Rosalia's choice is to be with that creep, Danny, nobody is chaining her to him."

"Yeah, well, you're not her mother."

"You're right, I'm not." My mother gave me a look like she wasn't above slapping me.

"But even if I was, Ma, I'd still say the same thing. She's made her choice. Nobody's forcing her to stay with him."

"Don't tell me what you'd do if you were somebody's mother, Carlos. You may be smart, but you're not smart enough to raise a kid. But I did think you had a heart, and I thought you loved your sister."

"Don't go there, Ma," I told her. "Don't start with that I-thought-you-loved-your-sister thing. It's unfair and crazy, and you know it."

Besides, our apartment was not that big. I heard Rosalia the same as Ma did when she came in at night and cried until she fell asleep. I heard her and I knew Ma heard her. Believe me, I looked closely for bruises when I talked to her. If I saw any, I knew I had to do something, even though I wasn't sure what. But as hard as it was to listen to her crying, if all the tears were about him cheating or generally being Mister Pigman, there wasn't anything I *could* do about that except try to get through to Rosalia when she gave me half a chance. And that wasn't often. Even when it had been a night when she'd been crying so loud that Ma had gone in, Rosalia had refused to say anything other than that they'd had an argument, but everything would be fine and she was sorry she woke Ma up. And the next day she'd go back for more.

I couldn't believe the three of us were so different. Every time I teased Ma about why she didn't want to date, she said, "Why don't I go out with a guy at my age? Because I don't have the patience to put up with any bull. And goin' out with somebody is about patience. Don't get me wrong," she'd say, "I got my wants. I'm human. But I'm not willing to put up with any crap. And as soon as any guy ever raised his voice to me at this point in my life, I'd put him in the hospital, and then where would I be?"

Rosalia wouldn't let go of a guy who was capable of putting *her* into the hospital, and I just wanted a guy! Not that

I would let anybody abuse me. I thought, *There has to be a way to know when you're dating somebody if they're capable of it. There have to be signs.* And even if there aren't, once the first fist is raised—don't you have enough sense to call it quits? *No, Carlos,* I told myself, there are thousands of statistics that tell you people don't have enough sense to call it quits. Still, I couldn't imagine myself being attracted to anybody with a mean streak. I tried to picture Gleason Kraft raising his arm to me like he was going to hit me—and I had to admit, as much as I liked him, no matter how cute or talented he was, I'd never allow him to cause me physical pain.

Ma told me, "I was watching a show called *Stop in the Name of Love* with this psychologist named Dr. Sydney. She was talking about doing this thing called an intervention. What it means is that people who have friends or family who are doing things like drinking themselves to death or eating and throwing up or *lettin' somebody beat the crap out of 'em* sit down with the person and they talk to 'em and tell 'em they have to change—or else."

"Ma, I know what an intervention is. But ganging up on Rosalia about that idiot is not going to do anything but make Rosalia cry and get mad at both of us, and who needs either one?"

"Look, Carlos, you're supposed to be the man of the house. Can't you act like one for once in your life?"

It was like she hit me as hard as Danny could ever have hit Rosalia. I felt tears immediately fill my eyes. I couldn't look at her. I tried not to even think about what she meant. It was too confusing. It hurt too much. I took a second so my voice wouldn't come out weird, and I said, "What is it exactly that you want me to do, Ma?"

I could tell she was sorry. When I finally got the guts to look at her, she looked like she had tears in her eyes too.

"I just don't want either one of you getting hurt. That's all."

"I know," I said quietly.

"I want us to sit down with her and tell her that if she breaks up with this guy it won't be the end of the world." She stopped for a second. The she said, "But if she keeps going out with him and he puts another mark on her face, I'm gonna—"

"I know, Ma. You already said what you were gonna do." Is that what she meant by the man of the house? Was I supposed to keep threatening what I was gonna do to him for hitting my sister?

Of course I was. I knew it, and I felt ashamed and embarrassed and scared. What I also knew was that even when those guys had attacked me, I hadn't defended myself. How could I be expected to defend Rosalia?

So what was I going to do to help the situation? To be the *man* of the house my mother was asking me to be?

"So when do you want to have this intervention?" The only thing more horrifying would be trying to fight Danny and his thugs.

"I don't think we should wait. I think if she comes home tonight all upset, we should talk to her, lay it right out there."

"Ma, she never comes right home. And I have to get up early in the morning, and so do you." Even though I was going to go ahead with this, I didn't want to face a scream-cry fest at one in the morning.

Ma gave me one of her looks, but I wasn't sure what it meant. Then I figured out she was considering the options. "I'll tell you this," she said. "If she comes home and I hear her crying, we're doing it *tonight*. This is where it stops. Do I have your word, Carlos?"

Ma never asked for my word on anything. When she asked me to do something, I usually did it. I almost never resisted. This was the first time in a very long time. And I knew she was right that we had to try to do something even if I didn't think this intervention idea was the best solution.

"Yes, Ma. You have my word."

Ma stared at me for a minute. "It's the right thing," she said. "We're her family."

Yeah, and again I thought, *We couldn't be more different. I guess I should be proud we're all as close as we are. There are kids in school who never see their families and a few who don't know who they even are. So, I guess I'm lucky.*

I wondered if getting rich and famous would mean it would be easier to protect my mother and sister. Could I arrange it so Ma never had to work, so she could never get laid off? I wasn't sure I could get that rich. And what about Rosalia? Wasn't she still young enough to be able to change jobs if she was working at one where there were creeps—but that wasn't the point with her, was it? There were creeps anywhere if that's what you were attracted to. No, I decided. It wasn't the money that would have any effect on Rosalia. But would an intervention at one in the morning?

Chapter 22

Rosalia came home right after work. Ma and me had made our deal that if she came home at one or one thirty and we heard her in her room crying as usual, we'd do our intervention. When she came in early, I was in my room, and Ma was in the living room. I listened to see if Ma was gonna start in on Rosalia anyway, but she didn't. I knew Ma was all prepared to play a combination of Oprah and The Godfather. When Rosalia went right to her room and didn't make a sound, I knew the intervention was canceled, thank God. Or at least postponed. Ma and me agreed, or at least she *made* me agree, that if we heard Rosalia coming in and crying again at all from now on, we'd still speak to her. So, all I could do was hope it didn't happen.

At around ten the next morning, I was at my locker whining to Angie about my whole career being destroyed by the Wicked Valentino when my cell rang. It was the store number. "Speaking of the Wicked Valentino," I said to Angie. "I shouldn't have said anything out loud. He probably saw me talking about him in his crystal ball. Now I'm gonna pay. Hello," I said in the most innocent voice I could get out.

"Hi, honey. It's Lissette."

"Oh, hi, Lissette." Angie smiled as if to say, *See, you're wrong. It's not Valentino at all.* But I shook my head to Angie. It still couldn't be anything great.

"Listen," Lissette said, "Valentino wanted me to call you. It's about this weekend."

What was he going to do, lay me off? Tell me they didn't need me till further notice? He couldn't. There were people who came in on the weekends especially to see me. Mostly women, but even some guys. I had a following. And the bottom line was, as the Wicked One liked to say himself, I made FeatureFace money. As a makeup artist, I wasn't supposed to ring up sales myself. But I still got credit for them if I sold a product to a client as a result of what Valentino called "consultations with practical application." That was a really confusing way of saying I put makeup on them from start to finish, telling them what I was doing along the way, and selling my brains out every time I said, "And this particular shadow looks good on your eyes because of how it brings out the flecks of green," or "I can't believe you're not using a concealer. Don't you see what an incredible difference it makes? And just so you know, we have a special on FeatureFace concealer this weekend only, so you're lucky that you came up to the counter and we met today. Because this is going to change the way your makeup looks from now on." I'd sold tons of FeatureFace that way. And I knew it.

"What about this weekend, Lissette?"

"Valentino was supposed to go out to Hollow Hills, New Jersey, to do a special appearance, but he said he wants you to go instead."

Whew! It definitely wasn't as bad as I expected. I wasn't

getting fired. I wasn't even getting "laid off." True, if I didn't know better, I might have been fooled by the whole "guest appearance" thing. If it had happened the first or second week I was there, I might have been so flattered, I'd have been screaming up and down the hallways of Sojourner Truth. But like I said, I knew better. Ever since I'd worked for FeatureFace, Valentino had talked about how awful going to another store was, especially if it was outside the city. "You have to get up extra early to catch some train or bus or both to some cow patch in Long Island, just because they're trying to boost sales. And you stand there while these families of thirteen come in, and you have to make up the mother, the grandmother, the daughter, and the auntie all the while knowing they're not going to buy an eyebrow pencil. And at the end of the day, you crawl to the bus that takes you to the train, and you get home at midnight, but you're too tired to do anything, so what is it for? Nothing. It's punishment." So, if Valentino considered this punishment, that's exactly what he was dishing out to me.

"Did you say *Hollow Hills*, New Jersey, Lissette?"

"Yes. That's where the store is." The whole time Angie was watching and listening, trying to figure out just how bad the situation was.

"Where is that, Lissette? I've never heard of it."

"Wait a minute, honey. I'll ask Valentino." *I can't believe what a creep he is that he won't even get on the phone and give me my punishment directly. He's probably standing right there next to her, grinning like a maniac.*

"I gotta go," Angie told me with a look of sympathy on her face. "Let me know what happens."

"I will, Ange," I said, even though I know she's only

going to the snack machine to see what she's going to eat through her next class.

"Carlos, honey?" Lissette was back.

"I'm right here, Lissette."

"Valentino says you should call the store and get directions."

Now, no matter what I thought he was trying to do, I was starting to get annoyed. How much of an idiot was he going to be?

"They didn't give him the directions, Lissette?"

"He said you should call the store," she repeated. I'd seen Lissette in situations like this before. Valentino used her like his puppet, and when she got confused about what to do next, she started to sound desperate. Still, if I was going to serve my time out in Hollow Hills, New Jersey, I had to at least figure out how to get out there, didn't I?

"So, it's Macy's in Hollow Hills, Lissette?" I was determined to sound calm, as though it made perfect sense and I was even happy to go. I wouldn't give Valentino the satisfaction of knowing that I knew how stinky my weekend was going to be.

"Yes, that's right, Carlos."

"And is it for both Saturday and Sunday?"

"No. Val says it's only for Saturday."

"Well, what about Sunday?" I was supposed to work both days in New York. What was he trying to pull?

"Val said because you're only part-time and you're getting a higher rate for Saturday as a guest artist, you can't come in on Sunday." I could only hope the guest artist rate was the same as my two-day salary. If it wasn't, it was really a low trick to pull on me.

"Okay. Well, you tell him thank you for me, Lissette. I'm so excited. Tell Valentino I said thank you for the opportunity."

"Okay, honey." I could tell she was relieved. She'd done her boss's dirty work and it had gone smoothly. He wouldn't be snapping at her like he did until it made me want to jump in and defend her. "See you soon," I told her, hoping it was true.

"Bye, Carlos," she said, sounding sad. Why couldn't she have said "Yes" when I said "See you soon"? Did she know something I didn't know?

chapter 23

Both Wednesday and Thursday nights, Rosalia came home by midnight, which meant she had to be coming straight home. I was relieved, and so was Ma. But I was also curious.

Friday afternoon I caught her just as she was leaving for her shift. "Rosalia," I said, trying to sound casual, "what's going on? You've been coming home so early—for you, at least."

"Yeah? You waiting up for me, Carlos?"

"No. I'm a light sleeper. You know that. I always wake up when you come home. So I look at the clock. I can tell you've been early."

"That's really spooky, Carlos. It sounds like you're trying to play Dad with me or something, and that is sooooo not like you." She was being a little nasty, and I heard it.

"I'm not playing Daddy, Rosalia. I was curious. I admit it."

"About what? You waiting for me to tell you I broke up with Danny? Is that it?"

I couldn't help myself. "Did you?"

Rosalia was putting on lipstick. I'd supplied her with enough testers and freebees to last her a lifetime.

"No."

"But you haven't been going out after work?"

Rosalia put on another coat of FeatureFace's Love Those Lips Gloss, which was enough for her to slide down the street on, and I could see her hand was shaking.

"Look, Miss Busybody—"

"Don't go there, Ro," I told her. My rule was that nobody calls me Miss unless I give them permission and I don't give anybody permission to call me anything except Carlos or Carrlos or great or fabulous or genius or beyond genius.

"All right!" She was still applying lip gloss. I wanted to snatch it from her. "Danny's not allowed back in Burrito Village because Miguel decided that it really was Danny who stole some of the money—even though he's *wrong*—"

"Who's wrong? Danny or Miguel?" I wanted to see if she was so far gone that she actually believed Danny was innocent.

"Miguel, of course." She glared at me. "Why am I telling you? Of course *you* believe Danny's some big thief. Why am I even saying anything to you about it?"

"You know what, Ro? I don't actually care if he stole the money or not. My concern is you. I asked you if you broke up, and you said no. So there's my answer."

"So you don't care if he's accused of something he didn't do and lost his job for it?"

"Not really. Rosalia, it's no surprise to you that I don't like Danny. I don't care if he stole or he didn't steal as long as you don't get accused of it."

"I'm sure that's next. Miguel has been treating me like

crap ever since he fired Danny, and looking at me all suspicious like he thinks I really did help him steal, and I'm about two seconds away from quitting that dumb job!"

"Oh, that makes perfect sense! You quit your job because your boyfriend gets fired for stealing and you don't like the way your boss looks at you even though he definitely could have fired you if he wanted to, if he was that suspicious. I mean, no offense, Ro, but it's Burrito Take-Out Village. I don't think he thinks you're going to take him to court for firing you unfairly."

"But I could. And it would serve his ass right."

I glanced at the clock. "Well, if you're not going to quit tonight, I suggest you get going. I'm going to the day care center, and I'm definitely late. Let's get out of here."

While we were walking to the door, I said, "It still doesn't explain why you're coming home so early. Is it because Danny doesn't have any money that you guys can't go out?" Which was probably not the case, because I knew with a guy like Danny, Rosalia probably paid for a lot of what they did anyway.

By that time we were outside the apartment, and I was locking the door. Rosalia made this big sigh and started for the stairs. "What?" I said.

"Why do you have to know everything, Carlos? Is this for you or for Ma? I bet it's for Ma."

"It's for me, Ro! Isn't it possible that I care enough to want to know how you're doing and that you're okay?"

"Fine," she said. And I knew the truth was finally on its way out. "Danny and I had a fight about the whole stealing thing and him getting fired, and he said he didn't have to explain anything to me, and . . ." Rosalia didn't cry a lot in front of people. Me and Ma heard her in her room, but even if we'd barged in, Rosalia would've denied she'd been crying. I'm sure she thought it was a sign of weakness, and she hated weakness, which is why I didn't get the attraction to Danny. She certainly wasn't stupid enough to mistake acting like a goon for strength, and if he was a thief, too, did she think that was being strong? Anyway, she stopped herself because she was about to cry, and I had a feeling it was going to be big if she let it out. So she wasn't going to.

I didn't push it. We were halfway down the stairs when she stopped and said in a very low, quiet, calm voice—almost as though she was someone else talking, "He told me he didn't want to see me anymore. Which is bull, because I see him all the time. He makes sure of it. And he's always with some ugly, trampy girl. . . . And that's the way it is."

Her eyes were full, but I knew she wouldn't let one tear drop. So I tried to match her calmness when I said, "I know you don't want me to say anything bad about him, so I won't. I don't understand why you care. I just want you to be all right." And then I added, "Safe."

"I'm safe, all right," she said in this weird voice, as though she was being sarcastic or as though whatever she wasn't saying was more important than what she *was* saying. But what I guessed she *was* saying was that, of course she was safe. Danny wasn't close enough to her physically for her to be anything but safe. But she still hurt. And for that, I was sad for her.

Chapter 24

Getting to Macy's in Hollow Hills was like a trek through the desert without water. Of course, I had to worry about being on time. I had to get up when most kids my age were just going to bed after a hard Friday night of partying. I gave my eyes and cheeks a little wake-up glow, courtesy of FeatureFace, so I wouldn't scare anybody at the store, and threw on my biggest dark glasses.

The train to Hollow Hills was the easiest part. I was nervous about making sure I got off at the right stop, but other than that, no problem. I was holding the notes from the lovely girl I'd talked to at the FeatureFace counter when I called for directions. She told me, while she popped gum in my ear, "Well, I never came here from New York, but I can ask somebody." Several long minutes later, the serial gum popper got back on and said, "I'm not sure which train it is, but you take the train to Hollow Hills, (pop) then when you get to the station, (pop) you have to catch two buses. I hope you like bus rides, (pop) 'cause you got two long ones ahead of you once you get off the train, and if you miss the first one, you may as well forget it (pop)."

I got off the train clutching my little note. It said, "Catch the first bus across the street from the train station. If it's already there, great. If it's not, it could be anywhere from a half hour to forty-five minutes before another one comes. Make sure it says 'Midtown.'"

I saw three buses across the street when I got off the train. I almost got hit running across to where they were, and the first one in line took off just as I leaped onto the sidewalk. I didn't see what it said on the front. All I could do was hope it wasn't the Midtown bus. The second bus said Port Beach, so I ran to the third. *Please let this be it.* And it was—MIDTOWN! With about twenty people standing in line, waiting to get on it. I knew if there were no seats and I had to *kneel*, I'd get on that bus. I had about forty-five minutes before the store opened, and I was supposed to be there behind the counter and ready to greet the Hollow Hills public.

When I'd called the store in Hollow Hills, the woman I talked to at the counter said to me, "Oh, you're the makeup artist! I never heard of a name like Valentino before. Is that your real name?"

And of course I had to tell her, "No, as a matter of fact, Valentino isn't coming. I thought he let the store know. Is the manager there?"

With her mouthful of gum, she said, "I am the assistant manager in training. The manager isn't here. She's on vacation this week. Why? Is there some kind of problem? Why isn't Valentino coming? I thought he was the one who was supposed to come."

"Yes . . . uh . . . er . . . he was, but he's unavailable, I think . . ." And then I thought, *The last thing I want to do now* is say the wrong thing and get into even more crap with Valentino. "All I really know is that he asked me to sub for him, so I am. I thought he called there, but I guess he didn't. I'm Carlos Duarte. I also work as a makeup artist for the New York store." When I heard myself say it, I felt really proud. It felt like I was saying, "I'm somebody too, you know. I'm as qualified as he is." And even if I was younger in the business than Valentino was, I did feel that way.

I started in again with, "So, if you could tell me how to get there," and that's when she told me about the train and two buses. And I understood why it was a good punishment from Valentino.

So I waited in line for the bus, dressed for work—but also for early travel—in my Gucci sunglasses (courtesy of Soraya's sale bin), my kelly green Alexander Wang knockoff bag, and my UGGs—which I wear to work, and then I change into my Kenneth Cole loafers. I was half nervous about getting to the store on time and still a little sleepy because I didn't get any rest. I tried to picture being a Guest Artist for the first time in a mall in New Jersey, and I couldn't. People around me were staring at me, which I was mostly used to. I didn't have on that much makeup and I thought I looked pretty conservative, but apparently I still stood out in the line waiting for the bus. However, I paid it no mind. I felt like a pioneer woman ready to board the covered wagon and head across the prairies of New Jersey to the Hollow Hills Mall.

I got on the bus and pulled out my MetroCard. I stuck it into the box and waited for it to register. Instantly, the driver said "That won't work."

"Excuse me," I said.

"Ya need a card for Jersey, miss." I heard "Jersey" and "miss." I've heard "miss" before, so I was more concerned about the card not being good. I didn't know how much money I had, and I definitely didn't know how much change. "If I don't have a card, do I need exact change?" I asked the driver.

"That's right," he said. And he looked up at me. I saw he realized I wasn't the "miss" he thought I was. I smiled at him like the passenger of the month as I dug in my bag for change. I had about ten dimes, five quarters, some nickels, and lots of pennies. I tried to put my fare together as fast as I could, but there were about twelve other people in line to get on the bus, and the line was getting longer by the second.

"Could ya step aside and let some otha people on," the driver barked at me.

"Yes, sir," I mumbled nervously. The old black lady sitting right behind him stared me up and down, and just when I thought she was going to make some awful crack, she said, "Take this." She held out her hand with the exact bus fare in it.

I told her, "I've got it right here. I'm sure of it. I can pay you back." I took her money, poured it into the coin slot, and then sat next to her and continued digging into my bag for the change to pay her back.

After I'd gathered enough change to give to her, she said loudly, "Keep all these pennies, baby. You can put them right back in your bag, 'cause I don't need all those pennies!" The two women across from her laughed, and the little girl that belonged to one of them said, "That boy has a big green purse," and followed that up with, "An' big, big ladies' sunglasses and girls' boots!" To which the old lady said, "The young ones will always tell the truth, won't they?

They're not scared, they don't try to hurt nobody's feelings, they just tell the truth!"

I started to go farther back to get away from the conversation about me from these people I didn't know, but I thought I should at least get the information about the second bus as long as I was so near the driver.

"Do you know what bus I take after this to get to the Hollow Hills Mall?" I asked the old lady.

"The mall?" she said. "No, I never been there. It's way out, isn't it?" She said to the woman across from her with the little girl.

"What's that?" the woman asked.

"The mall," the old lady repeated.

"That boy wants to go to the mall to buy a purse," the little girl said. "And probly some more ladies' sunglasses." I was not the best judge of brats, but I'd say she was about three going on forty.

"We're goin' out there," the woman with the little girl said. "Once we get to the midtown stop, you get off. Then the mall bus should be right there."

"The mall bus?" I asked quietly. I was trying not to attract any more attention than was necessary.

"Yep," the woman said. "It says, 'Mall' right on it." I was pretty sure she had to be wrong about what it said—what bus says "Mall" on it?—but I didn't question it. I thanked her.

"You follow us," she said, with the girl staring me up and down. "We're goin out there. We're getting on the same bus."

I thanked her again and I looked away quickly, because I knew the little girl was going to start to talk to me if I didn't. But it was too late.

"How come you got that big green purse?" she asked me.

"I've got a lot to carry," I said to her, giving her my Glinda the Good Witch smile and hoping she'd stop, but I knew she wouldn't.

"Why you got a girl's purse to carry your stuff?"

Okay, so the mother has been nice to me and I didn't want to cause a scene on the Hollow Hills bus, so I said as calmly as possible, "I think it's for both boys and girls." The old lady snorted. The mother pulled the girl by the shoulder and said, "Stop being so nosy. Mind your business," and I thanked God it was not going to get any worse.

We got to the midtown stop and got off, and like the woman said, the bus marked HOLLOW HILLS MALL was right there. I followed her and the little girl, who couldn't take her eyes off my bag. When they started to get on the second bus, she tripped up the stairs looking back at me, and I felt like I wanted to stick my tongue out at her or worse for embarrassing me on the first bus.

Once we were all on, the woman said to me, "Now it's not all that far from here. We'll probly get there right as the stores are opening." If that was true, it was good enough for me. Any later, and I'd be disappointed. I already had a reputation in the city for being ten minutes early, and I didn't want anybody in Hollow Hills reporting back to Valentino that I showed up late.

I stared out the window, thinking it looked *beyond suburban*. I wouldn't have been surprised if I had started seeing cows. We were on the highway, and it reminded me of going to Fresh Air Camp for the day and a half I did when I was ten. It was my ma's idea, and I tried to fight it, but once I got there, the Fresh Air family decided I was not the cute little Spanish boy they thought they were saving from the hot summer in grimy New York City. Mostly because I asked the mother of the family if I could try out her eye shadow. I don't see how it could have been anything else—I was extremely well-mannered. Even when I asked, I know I was polite about it. But I didn't feel all that comfortable anyway. The house was fabulous and the furniture was very tasteful and chic, but the father looked at me like I was a reptile, and he wouldn't talk to me, and the mother and daughter kept asking me what I did to make my hair so black and curly. And even though, yes, I wore bracelets and carried a little purse and was interested in cosmetics and hair products, I certainly wasn't dyeing my hair at ten. So, what were they thinking?

The first night, we all had dinner. The mother had on this smoky silver eye shadow that was probably the most exciting thing in the whole room. I got nuts about it and asked her right there at the dinner table if I could try some on, and the next morning she said to me (the father wouldn't speak to me at all), "Sometimes adults make mistakes, Carlos. And the good part of that is, it's never too late to correct them." And by dinnertime of that day, I was back in grimy New York City eating with Ma and Rosalia. When Ma asked me what happened, I repeated exactly what the mother had said to me about mistakes. Ma said, "Stupid Connecticut country snot! She's the one who needs some fresh air." And that was the last time we talked about it.

But I do think about it again on the way to the Hollow Hills Mall to be guest makeup artist for the day. I'm older and bigger, but I feel all of a sudden just like I did when I was being sent home from that family in Connecticut. Like a freak.

. . .

The mall looked like an island in the middle of nowhere surrounded by an enormous parking lot. There weren't that many cars, which made me wonder if it was a sign of how many people there'd be in the store. But because I always like to be optimistic, I told myself, *Don't worry, it's early. By noon there'll be thousands of people. The place will be mobbed.*

I was first in line to get off the bus. I could see from the window that Macy's was already open, and I was in a big hurry to get there. It was 10:10, and officially I was supposed to be there at ten. I thanked the woman who had been my guide from bus to bus, and just before I dashed across the parking lot to the store, I looked over my sunglasses and said a big "Bye-bye" to the little girl. She continued to stare at me as though it was going to be a while before all of her questions about me would be answered, so she was taking one final look.

Once I entered the mall, it was a fast-food wonderland—Pizza Hut, Darby's, Thai Express, Little Italy, Domino's, Caesarino's, Rib Shack, Steamers. Ohmygod. And there were people in all of them, pigging out before ten thirty in the morning!

I kept going, looking for Macy's. When I didn't see it, I panicked. Maybe this section was only for food? Not possible. Or was it? I ran into the Domino's and shouted, "Where's Macy's?"

The whole place stared, but one of the guys behind the counter pointed. I yelled, "Thanks!" and kept moving.

Finally, at the end of one of the glass corridors, I saw it. Hallelujah! Once I stepped through the doors, I was stunned at how few people were in the store. Opening on a Saturday morning in the city meant, as Valentino would say, "Time to greet the masses, dolls!" But here I could have set up a stage and done a tap number with all the Radio City Rockettes and we still would have outnumbered the customers.

I dropped my bag, pulled out my Kenny Cole loafers, and pulled off my UGGs. I wanted to make sure I looked professional when I walked up to the FeatureFace counter.

It took me a few minutes to find the cosmetics area. There weren't as many huge signs as in the city. FeatureFace was in the back next to men's underwear. I thought, *That makes perfect sense, I suppose—for a place called Hollow Hills! Selling makeup right next to boxers and briefs.*

The first thing that I saw was a sign announcing FEATUREFACE IS PROUD TO WELCOME CELEBRITY GUEST MAKEUP ARTIST VALENTINO! I cringed. *Well, here goes,* I thought. I threw my shoulders back and hitched my bag up on my shoulder, which made me feel stronger and more forceful. Just then a really young woman came up to me, popping gum like she could actually hear a beat in her head, and I thought it must be the girl who gave me directions on the phone. She was black and pretty, with huge fake eyelashes that reminded me of Lissette's—except that this girl was giving you *major Afro,* like from the eighties. She had a nose ring, and her black top was open so far down, her "girls" were speaking to me before she did.

"Are you Valentino?" she asked, and I was being surveyed like a piece of land up for sale, for the fiftieth time that morning.

"No. I spoke to someone on the phone, and thought I cleared that up. I'm Carlos Duarte. Valentino and I—"

"Oh, that's right," she said, "you're the substitute or the replacement or whatevah."

I rolled my eyes at her, and it happened so fast, I couldn't control it. But I hoped she didn't notice.

"I'm Nigeria. I'm the assistant manager in training."

"Then, it *was* you," I told her. "Of course. I remember your *title*." And of course she didn't get the read. But she extended her hand, which, of course, had to have the longest nails on record, curling over. With decals of purple and gold. I wanted to run in the other direction.

"Ain't nobody here but us," she said. "The manager, Carrie, is just like that old movie about that blond girl named Carrie with the red rabbit eyes who makes stuff happen just 'cause she thinks about it real hard. Crazy Carrie. So it's a good thing she's on vacation. She suffers from migraines. When she's not on vacation, she calls in every other day and says she got a migraine. I asked her why she don't go to the doctor and get it straightened out, and she say there ain't no cure for migraines. So whenever something happens here she can't handle, she gets all red in the face and says, 'I got a migraine,' and then she goes home. And calls in sick the next day. I wish somebody would fire her ass, so I could be manager and run this sucker like it should be run."

I couldn't even control my laughter. I started howling in the middle of the store at the FeatureFace counter no more than five minutes after I got there. And at first Nigeria was just smiling and saying, "I ain't lying. You think I'm lying, don't you?" Which only made me laugh more. But then she started laughing with me, and we were doubling over when the first client came up to the counter.

She was about 104 years old, but you could tell she had *beyond major* bucks. She said to us like she was the queen of Russia, "I called earlier this week to schedule an appointment with the makeup artist, and they told me I couldn't schedule one, I had to come in and it was first come, first serve or something ridiculous like that. So, is he here, this Valentino person?"

I really did think this was going to set Nigeria and me off even worse than we already were, but I think it was the professional in both of us that surfaced and we stopped laughing so quickly, you'd think the queen of Russia had just announced someone had died.

"*I'm* the guest artist for today." I said to the 104-year-old woman. I'd taken my sunglasses off, but she hadn't. They were Yves Saint Laurent, and not knockoffs, trust me. She had one of those long gray bobs, which you know meant she had always loved her hair and didn't want to cut it, no matter how old she was. She was wearing a sweater set and pearls. I didn't think anybody still wore sweater sets, but I guess rich older ladies in New Jersey do.

"*You're* Valentino?" she asked as though she was really saying, *I'm going to ask you once, and then I'm going to call the police and have you arrested for impersonating a real makeup artist.*

"No, I'm not Valentino, I'm Carlos Duarte and I also work in the New York store. Valentino was unable to make it today."

"Oh. Really."

I wanted to say, "Yes, really. Now get over it, 'cause I'm just as good as he is, if not better, so do you want me to make your old face up or not?" And I knew I could do a fabulous job, except I also knew the hardest part would be her attitude about it.

"What is it I can do for you today?" Out of the corner of my eye, I could see Nigeria watching the whole thing like it was a movie. Somehow, even though we'd just met, I could feel her support. Like they say, she had my back.

"But you're so young! I'm sure you're good at putting makeup on young girls your age, but for me, I don't know, I'm very disappointed. I thought they were sending someone with experience in the field. The paper said this Valentino worked with entertainment people and the like."

"And so have I," I said, throwing my head up and my shoulders back. "I guarantee you, ma'am, FeatureFace doesn't send people out to represent them unless they have a great deal of experience. And I certainly wouldn't qualify as a guest artist if I wasn't at the top of my profession." I couldn't believe what I was saying. It was like I was possessed. I actually sounded a little like Valentino. I think I was unconsciously imitating the way he sounded when a customer dared question his judgment about something. By the time he finished, they were willing to buy seven of what he'd recommended, even after they'd first doubted him. "But, of course, you have to be comfortable with the person who's working with you. I'd be happy to help you, if you think I can." I actually felt Nigeria give me a little nudge of support on my back.

The queen of Russia slowly took off her YSL sunglasses. She had piercing blue eyes that had a little sadness in them, and under them she had bags to her knees.

"The thing is, I have a brunch this afternoon. And it's with some friends I haven't seen in a very long time, so naturally I want to look my best. There's a makeup person at my hair salon, but he's so . . . difficult. I just really am not in the mood to argue with him. So I thought this would be an opportunity to have someone else do my makeup, and I suppose because of the ad and the reputation of the company, I thought, well, I'd give it a chance. If it didn't work, I could always run home, wash my face, and do what I always do. I'm not trying to look so very different from usual. I just wanted maybe to have an expert, you know . . . add a little something . . . and maybe help me with this . . . puffiness around my eyes."

Puffiness? Lady, you're walking around with an entire set of Louis Vuitton luggage under your eyes. And we're talking the real deal!

"I'm sure I can help you. Do you want to take a few minutes to think about it?" I wasn't going to give her a hard sell. Why should I? It wasn't going to be the easiest job in the world. But I was confident that I really could make a difference if she let me.

"No," she said, "I'm going to take a chance." I wanted to tell her not to bother. And Nigeria made this big "Hmmph" behind me as if she totally agreed.

"Do you do it right here, or is there somewhere we can go that's more private?" the queen of Russia asked me.

By this time Nigeria had had about all she was going to take. "No, he does it right here. It's the same with all the customers. You sit right here at the counter where all the makeup is, and he puts it on you. That's how it's done. There's no place else to go."

I had to stifle a little grin. I wouldn't have put it quite so bluntly. But it was the truth, and it was out. So there.

"Very well, then. Is this where I sit?" The woman gestured toward the stool at the counter.

"That's it," Nigeria said. She was having a ball letting this woman know who was boss. But if this woman was going to be our customer, I wanted to soften things up a bit so she'd feel comfortable.

"You relax for a second," I said to her gently. "Let me get my supplies. Oh, by the way, since we're going to be working together . . ." I stuck out my hand. "Carlos," I told her for the second time.

"I'm June Karakter," she said. "That's *K-A-R-A-K-T-E-R*." Again Nigeria snorted loudly, and again I had to stifle a giggle.

"Well, I'll be right back, June," I said, sounding like a nurse going to get a sedative.

Nigeria followed closely behind me as I went to the back counter to pull my smock out of my bag and pull some makeup from stock. "She's a character, all right. I don't care how she spells it. I don't know how you gonna do anything with that puss. This I gotta see!"

I shook my head at how funny she was and began pulling everything I'd need for surgery. "Prepare to be astonished, girl!" I said to her. And the two of us high-fived.

As I was doing June Karakter's makeup, I had a few customers come up out of curiosity, but it was really pretty quiet overall. I realized if I took my time with old June, I could not only do a miraculous job, but I could get her to buy lots and lots of products. For example, why she or the makeup artist at her salon had never put a concealer on those bags under her eyes, I couldn't figure out. Not only was it the obvious solution, but it looked like she'd had an eye lift within a total of ten minutes. I pulled over one of the counter mirrors and showed her what I'd done.

"I can't believe it," she said. "Whatever you did, I'd pay for you to come miles to do it again for the right occasion, and buy lots of whatever you used to do it with!" And wasn't that the point? So I was careful to talk her through each and every step as I usually did with clients, carefully pointing out the wonder of each FeatureFace product I was using.

When I was almost finished, June kind of whimpered in this soft, melting voice that was a little scary, "Carlos, I love the way your touch feels on my skin." I didn't know what to answer, so I thought maybe it was best not to say anything. When I was about to step back and tell her to take a look at the rejuvenated June, I realized several women were standing around me watching. One of them said, "If you can do that to *her*, I want you to do me next!" And the rest of them were chiming in, "Me too!" "Is there a sign-up sheet?" Not quite what I was used to in the city, but I got the point, and I was happy.

So was June. In fact, June was ecstatic. "This is incredible! You're incredible," she gasped. "I can't believe what you've done in such a small amount of time. I look like I've been on vacation!" And one of the women standing around said, "A long one!" Nigeria didn't even try to hide her laugh.

I had Nigeria ring up three hundred dollars' worth of makeup. If I didn't sell another lipstick, I'd done *beyond fabulous* for the day. Nigeria cracked, "Honey, we can close up and go home now. There are Saturdays I've been here and we've made a hundred dollars the whole day." June tried to give me a twenty-five dollar tip, but we're not allowed to take them. Instead I gave her a FeatureFace card with my name and number on the back and said, "All you have to do is call me, and I'll bring my bag of tricks and we'll get you ready for any occasion, night or day." She shook my hand and said, "You'll be my special weapon from now on! And if you lived in the area, I swear I'd put you on permanent retainer."

I went on to my next client, who I knew wasn't going to buy half as much as June, but I was definitely doing what I was supposed to—attract business and sell, sell, sell. After her there was a family—a mother, her twenty-year-old daughter, and a cousin with severe acne. When I'd finally finished my fight with the cousin's face, she said, "I'm so disappointed. I thought you wouldn't be able to see my pimples anymore." I said as quietly and as gently as I could, "You might want to consider seeing a dermatologist," and she looked at me as if I'd suggested plastic surgery. I just kept smiling at her, happy the family would be leaving the counter soon. I could have bet Nigeria a hundred dollars that the girl wouldn't make it out of the mall without grabbing a slice or a burger or a bag of fries to start a whole new crop of eruptions. Like I heard Valentino tell one of his customers once when she'd wrecked his nerves, "Some makeup artists are magicians, and I've been called one myself, but even I can't make some things disappear!"

Between the mother, the daughter, and the cousin, after full makeovers they bought one bottle of liquid foundation, and an eyeliner. I was exhausted and ready to go home. Even the time I'd had with June Karakter was a distant memory.

My cell rang, and when I looked to see who it was, I didn't recognize the number. In the New York store the rule was that you couldn't use your phone until your break, but I'd forgotten to turn it off when I started work that morning. I let it ring long enough for me to get to the back counter before answering it.

"Hello?"

"Carlos? Dear, it's Shirlena. Sweetie, I need you to do me a huge favor!"

Chapter 25

I felt a bolt of lightning go through me when I heard her voice. "Sure!" I said without any hesitation. What difference did it make? I would do anything Shirlena Day asked me to.

"You're a doll," she said. "But I want to tell you what it is, because if you can't do it, I'll understand completely and I promise I won't hold it against you."

Okay, so now I was convinced it was a practical joke. It was Angie, or Soraya, or somebody who knew about the Shirlena thing and knew that right now I had to be standing in the middle of Macy's in Hollow Hills, New Jersey, wetting my pants like a toddler. Where was the hidden camera?

"I'll do it," I laughed. "What is it?"

Shirlena laughed too. "I don't know what's gotten into Christian, my makeup guy, but he's been acting like a complete idiot ever since I told him I wanted you to help us figure out something to use on my face so I don't look like I've crashed a party in a beehive when it's all over. He said he called you. Did he?"

"He did. And I would have sent over the makeup, but he

didn't give me an address, so I was waiting for him to call me back."

"Well, the truth is, he came in once to do something, but he was in such a horrible mood that we had a fight and I . . . Let's just say, he is skating on very thin ice right now, and I don't even know if he'll show up for our taping on Monday night. So I was wondering if you could come by with the hyper- . . . hypa- . . ."

I thought she had to be kidding. "Hypoallergenic makeup," I told her. But then it sunk in. *Come by?* "Did you say you wanted me to come by with it? Come by where?"

"The studio. When we tape. I figure if he shows, great. If he doesn't, if you can come early enough, there's another makeup person here who knows how to do my makeup, and you can give her the nonallergic stuff, and between the two of you, you can figure out how to mix it or substitute or whatever you have to do. Would you be willing to do that? They'll pay you, of course."

All right, so it wasn't a joke. I knew that already. It's just that it didn't feel like my life, either. My dream life, sure. Absolutely. But my real life? Shirlena Day was calling me to ask if I could bring makeup to her studio and help another makeup artist figure out what to use on her for a national television show.

"Of course I'd be willing to do it. I've seen the show a hundred times"— All right, so I'd seen it maybe five times, but there was YouTube, wasn't there?—"so I know I could figure out how to replace the stuff that's giving you a reaction. The only thing I'm not totally sure about is your Michelle O character."

Shirlena laughed. "Don't sweat Michelle, honey. With her the wig is the key. Once I've got my Michelle O wig on, the incredible actress that I am takes over. Now, here's the address. You can come and play, and I'll tell Paulette, the other makeup artist, you'll be here."

I stood there writing down the address of the studio where *Smokin' Friday Nights* was taped. Actually, I was tap-dancing, a combination of nerves and excitement. I heard Nigeria out front telling a customer that I'd be with her in a minute to do her makeup. She came back to the section of the counter where I was on the phone with Shirlena. "You got fans out there, Mr. Guest Artist. It don't matter that Valentino isn't here. The word has gone all over the store that the FeatureFace guy is fabulous! And they're lining up. So you better get your butt out there."

I got off the phone, and every part of me was tingling. It kind of reminded me of when I was ten and got frostbite, except the frostbite went from intense tingling to intense pain, and so far, this was only the tingling part. But I was already thinking that in order for the dream to reach *beyond miraculous*, I had to make sure everything went smoothly and professionally so there'd be no doubt in Shirlena's mind that I was a *makeup genius*! Since it was already Saturday, and I was supposed to be on the *Smokin' Friday Nights* set Monday—just thinking about the words "on the set" started my tingles up again—I had to go to the New York store on Sunday. I had to pick up the whole line of FeatureFace hypoallergenic products, called FeatureFace Free-Zone, plus whatever other brushes or pencils I might need. That way, I could go to sleep Sunday night—fat chance—knowing I had everything I needed for Monday at the studio.

Shirlena had said my "call" was at five thirty, which meant I could go by the day care center after school, work for maybe an hour, and then go uptown to the studio. I didn't even have to shop for something new, because I already had the perfect outfit picked out. I'd wear my almost-skinny black jeans, purple T-shirt, and my black YSL sport jacket from Soraya's sale box last year. Oh, and my black stone crucifix for sure. One, it was the *only* accessory for every important occasion, and two, if there was ever a time to have a crucifix around my neck for protection and good spirits, it would be Monday night.

I went back out to the front of the counter, where Nigeria was making excuses for me. Another girl had shown up late for work, so she was handling some of the sales, but what Nigeria had said was true. The word had spread that this guy at the FeatureFace counter was doing makeup and it was fabulous. So the line never stopped until it was six o'clock and the store was about to close. I said as politely as I could to the last two girls in line, "Sweethearts, I'm sure you two do everything together, don't you?" And they giggled and answered "Yes" in a chorus. And I said, "Well, then, the best thing for you to do is come back together the next time I'm here. Because today I have enough time to do only one more face, and if I do that, one of you is going to be very jealous."

And now, of course, one of them said, "Can't you just do both of us really quick, pleeeez?" I could feel Nigeria about ready to step in and give the girls her own special good-bye, but I didn't want to end the day that way. I said to Nigeria, "Hon, can you please get me two of our special Blush in a Rush samples?" Nigeria looked at me like, *I have no idea what* this game is, but if you expect me to play, I don't know how. So, I said, "Never mind, hon. I'll get them." I went to the back counter and pulled two tiny pots of sample blush, Scotch-taped a card with my name written on it, and brought them back out. "Here you go, girls! We aren't really supposed to give out free makeup unless someone has made a purchase, but because you two are so sweet and look so disappointed, I'm giving them to you with my card attached, so that when you are in our New York City store, you can ask for me and I will drop whatever I'm doing and give you the makeup session I can't give you right now!" They bought it. I think it was having the little presents, and that's what I'd counted on. I'd watched Valentino shoo people away when it was time to close, and I'd always thought, *Ya gotta give 'em something if you want 'em to come back!* So now it was my turn to do exactly that.

Both of them chimed "Thank you" and went off looking like they'd scored. Nigeria said, "Sorry I missed the hint, but that was on the money! You know how to work a customer, don't you? I definitely learned a thing or three from you today."

After I packed, we exchanged numbers and hugged. I told Nigeria if she ever moved to the city, I'd love to work with her at the New York store. I knew Valentino would have a lot to say about those nails with the purple and gold decals and her rough language. But I also could tell that the chances of Nigeria moving to New York were small. She loved New Jersey and hated the idea of what she called, "gettin' pushed in and outta subways and all over the street by total damn strangers."

I stood at the entrance to the mall parking lot, where the bus stop was, and watched Nigeria as she got into her little green car. "This is my baby," she said. "You think I could afford to keep her in the city? Hell, no! And you think I'd give her up after wanting a car since I was four? Hell to the no again!" It was so funny to me how different we were.

"Hey, Carlos, man, you wanna hang out with me for a little while before you go home? I'll drive you to the bus stop after."

Any other time I would have said yes. I loved Nigeria, she was my girl. I wished I could have her as my friend in the city. She was older than Angie and Soraya, or at least she acted a lot older. But, as different as we were, the thing I liked about her most was that she was telling the whole world, just like I was, *There's only one of me—so you better be ready!*

But my other girl's voice, Shirlena's, was in my head, and I couldn't wait to get back to the city to figure out what I needed for Monday and the studio taping.

"All right, then, Boo. Later. Remember Nigeria!"

She drove off, waving and blasting her speakers. It was Alicia Keys singing, "Have you ever tried sleeping with a broken heart?" Nigeria was wailing and bobbing her head, waving her hands with those nails in the air. "Ooooooh, have you ever . . ."

And I wondered if Nigeria had ever had to sleep with a broken heart. I could hear her telling me, "Yo, Man, Carlos, are you for real? Of course I have."

Of course I would have wanted to know all the details. Who, when, what her makeup looked like that last time she'd seen the guy and what she'd do if she had a second chance.

If I'd known what was waiting for me at home, I might have decided to stay in New Jersey, hanging out with Nigeria. But to tell you the truth, I know now I could only have put it off for so long.

chapter 26

"You tell your brother that lie and see if he believes you!" As soon as she heard my key in the door, Ma started to include me. I'd heard her from the time I started up the stairs to the sixth floor. She was screaming like the house was on fire, and to her the situation was worse than that.

"I'm not telling him nothing. I already told you, and if you don't believe me, then what sense does it make to keep saying it?"

"Because you're not telling the truth! And part of me says, 'Who cares what she says? Just go do what you have to do. Go make that guy look as bad as your daughter looks. Only worse!' "

That's what I walked into. The whole apartment felt like a war zone. Ma was in the living room, and Rosalia was in her bedroom.

"You go in there and take a look at her and see if she tells you the same lie she told me!"

I looked at my mother. Neither her nor Rosalia were women I wanted to mess with ever. Ma could be a marine sergeant—not that I knew that much about them, but she was my worst nightmare of one—and Rosalia was definitely her mother's daughter. She could turn on you and make you think she seriously might pull a weapon. Fortunately, I'd never had her that mad at me, but I'd seen her in that frame of mind, and it was scary. That's why it was hard to imagine her taking so much crap off this Danny creature.

"What's going on?" I asked Ma, even though I knew. I really did not want to be in the middle of this. I wanted to take my phone, go back outside to Dunkin' Donuts, buy a cup of tea, and sit in peace, making out my list of all the stuff I needed for Monday.

"You go take a look at her and you ask *her* what's going on."

Okay. I knew better than to press it with Ma. So I went to Rosalia's door and knocked. "Hey. What's going on?"

"Nothing. Leave me alone."

Ma was right behind me. She called in to Rosalia, "Open the door, Rosalia, and let your brother see what that bastard did to you. I'm gonna kill him. I swear I'm gonna kill him!"

"Ro, what happened? Did he hurt you?"

"I told Ma and she won't believe me. Stupid Miguel was mopping the floor, and I was running around like crazy because we were so busy, and I slipped and fell. I hit my face on the corner of the stove and I got a little mark on my cheek, and now Ma's going crazy saying it was Danny."

"Let your brother see your face, Rosalia! Open the door and let him see it."

"No!" Rosalia yelled back. "I wish you'd stop. I told you I don't even see Danny anymore. He's going out with some-body else. I told you that."

"I don't believe you," Ma said, still shouting to the

closed door. "I don't believe you for one second. And if you don't open the door right now, I'm going to find that piece of crap and tell him if he wants to beat on a woman, I dare him to try it with *me!*"

Ma left Rosalia's door and started walking toward the apartment door. Immediately Rosalia opened her door. I stared at her cheek. It was red and bruised badly.

"Please. Rosalia, tell me the truth. Did he do that to you?" I knew what I wanted her to answer, even though I also knew I wouldn't believe her.

"I swear. I swear it wasn't Danny. I haven't seen him in weeks. He doesn't come around, he doesn't call me, I haven't seen him. He didn't touch me."

By now Ma was back. "Why do you lie for him? Why don't you tell the truth?" She turned to me, "Carlos, you look at her face. You tell me. Do you believe this stupid story about slipping on the floor and hitting the stove?"

I took a deep breath. No, I didn't believe for a second that Rosalia hit her face on a stove at work. And if she had, Rosalia would have been the first to talk about trying to sue so she'd be rich enough to buy her own apartment. But I didn't want to tell Ma what I believed, because I knew she was ready to go into the streets and try to find Danny. This was it. She was finished even pretending she believed Rosalia. And even if she didn't find him, which would probably be the case, she wouldn't be satisfied until she had. So no, I wasn't going to stand there and throw gasoline on the fire by saying, "Ma, you're right. It looks like Danny hit Rosalia, no matter what she says."

Instead I thought hard and fast. And what I came up with was, "Ma, I have to talk to you."

Ma and Rosalia both looked surprised. "What do you mean you have to talk to me?" Ma said.

"I have to speak to you. Please." I said it as forcefully as I could.

Ma looked at me for a second. Then she looked at Rosalia. In the moment of silence I knew I had a chance to do what I wanted even though I hadn't thought it completely through.

"Come here." I turned and walked toward the kitchen. Ma slowly followed.

When I got there, I turned to her and looked into her scowling eyes.

"Ma," I said, just above a whisper, "please. I want you to do something for me."

"What are you talking about?" she asked me. She was still upset, but her voice was almost as low as mine.

"I want you . . . to let me handle this."

"What are *you* going to do?"

"*Please.* Just trust me. If I don't take care of it, then . . . fine. But give me a chance."

Ma was still breathing fire. The only thing I had going for me was that I sounded like I knew what I was going to do, like I really had a plan.

"I don't know," she said. "I'm fed up with this. I'm telling you, Carlos, if I have to look at one more bruise, I don't care what they do to me, but he'll never put his hands on my daughter again, so help me!"

"I know, Ma! Don't you think I know? But you have to trust me. You have to!"

Ma stared at me. Big noisy breaths were coming out of her like she was having some kind of attack, asthma or something. "All right. You fix it. But you better fix it good." She went to the kitchen window and stared out of it. I could still hear her thick breathing.

I went back to Rosalia's room. She was waiting at the door.

I pushed her into her room and shoved the door closed. I kept my voice even and as calm-sounding as I could.

"Why do you keep lying about this, Ro? Have you looked at your face? He's going to kill you!"

"I'm not lying and he's not going to kill me. Why do you and Ma keep saying that? Do you think I *would* let somebody hurt me and not do anything?"

I looked at her. I realized there wasn't any use. I looked at the bruise on her cheek, and I looked into her eyes and realized she was going to continue to lie. Why? I didn't know, but I did know she would, no matter what Ma or I said.

I knew I had to do something, but I wasn't sure what. I also knew I had to figure it out fast.

chapter 27

I didn't sleep that night, and I couldn't wait to get up the next morning. I wanted to go over my list, which I'd done a thousand times during the night, and make sure I had everything I needed for the Shirlena Day taping. I also couldn't get the picture of Rosalia's face out of my mind, with my mother screaming at her.

What was I supposed to do, hire a hit man? I mean, I knew that's what Ma was about two seconds away from doing. And I knew if I didn't think of something fast, she would probably resort to doing that or committing assault and battery with her own hands.

But until I figured it out, I had to keep moving. I got up, went over my list for the thirty-third time, showered, and dressed. Then I tried to figure out my biggest problem in the next few hours—how to tell Valentino what I was going to do with Shirlena, and get his okay. Even "his okay" seemed like a stretch when I thought about it. He'd never be all right with it. So how could I get the makeup I needed out of the store for Monday if I had to get his permission to do it?

It was especially hard since Valentino *never* worked on

Sundays. Lissette would be there. She worked every hour he'd give her, because, as she said, "It takes a whole lotta dollas to look like you're makin' a good living, and I'm trying to at least *look* like I'm makin a good living."

And this kid, Mirta, who Valentino hired for weekends only, would be there. But no Valentino. And I didn't want to wait until Monday, because that was too close. If everything didn't go right, I'd have to try to reach Shirlena at the last minute and tell her so, and that would be *beyond humiliating.* So my plan was to go to the store and call Valentino from there with as much confidence as I could fake. I'd sound as though I was so sure he'd be all right with me leaving the store with the makeup that, it was only a formality that I even let him know.

Before I left the apartment, Ma cornered me. "You remember what you said, Carlos, about this thing with your sister. I'm depending on you."

"Yeah, Ma. I remember." I left the house shaking. Rosalia. Ma. Valentino. I could only handle one thing at a time.

When I got to the store, Lissette had a thousand questions about the Hollow Hills Mall. "Did you have fun? Did you have any customers? Did you make them any money? Or was it as awful as Valentino says? Would you ever go back again? Why do you look so terrible? Is it because you hated the Mall so much, or because you don't have on any makeup?"

"First of all, Missy Lissy, about the makeup thing—I may have a little glow going when I come in here—if I didn't, these store lights would kill me, I'd look like the bride of

Frankenstein—but I don't wear *makeup* makeup! I stopped doing that when I was in junior high school! So looking awful because I don't have any on? You must be thinking of someone else. And, yes, I enjoyed myself at the Hollow Hills Mall. It was *beyond fabulous*. And even though I hope to never go back there, I wouldn't be really upset if I had to, because they loved me and I loved them."

Then I got right down to business. "Now, listen, Lissette. I have to talk to you, and I'm hoping you're the friend I think you are, because if you aren't, I could be committing suicide."

"Oooo, hon, that's a lot for a Sunday morning," Lissette said, looking worried. "Even Valentino doesn't come in with that much drama this early on a Sunday morning."

"That's because Valentino doesn't ever come in on a Sunday morning. And he doesn't ever come in early at all. Seriously, Lissette, what I have to tell you is of the utmost importance. Do you think you can handle it?"

Lissette flicked back her hair. "I don't know anything I *can't* handle." Then she told Mirta, "Hon, could you watch the front of the counter for a second? We're going in the back for a *business* chat." I knew she said "business" so Mirta could never tell Valentino that she was just gossiping at the back counter on FeatureFace time.

As soon as we got back there, she stuck her face close to mine. "What is it? What'sthematter?"

I started with what she already knew—that Shirlena had come in and talked to me about her makeup for *Smokin' Friday Nights* and we'd hit it off. Then I continued with the call from Christian, her makeup guy, and how he'd never followed up. Finally I told her how Shirlena had called me while I was working at Hollow Hills, and how she wanted me to work with her for the taping the next night.

"Oh, baby, baby, babeeeee!" she squealed, and tossed that weave back and forth like she was preparing for takeoff. "I'm nobody's fool! I can see how talented you are, Carlos! And I could see how you and Shirlena got along!" She stopped and looked down at the floor, then back up at me. It was as though she was a big, pretty brown balloon—with a lot of hair—and someone had stuck a pin in it.

"The thing is, I don't see Valentino exactly telling you, 'Go on, take all the makeup you want and you go work on Shirlena's makeup, when that's what I been workin' my butt off for all these months.' That, I just don't see happening!"

"I know," I said. "Me either."

"Ooooweee, he's gonna be mad!" Lissette seemed to be enjoying this part almost too much. "He'll be so jealous!"

"Do you think he'll fire me?"

"How's he gonna fire you? You didn't do anything wrong. The most he could do is figure out some way to send your butt back to Hollow Hills Mall, but you said you didn't mind it that much, so that wouldn't be all that bad to you."

"It would be horrible if it was permanent, that's for sure. So I don't think I have any choice. I think I have to call Valentino, tell him the truth, and take my chances."

Lissette shook her head slowly. "I think you should come up with something else. Even if he doesn't send you to a mall somewhere, he could make your life so miserable here, you'd hate it. Or, because you're part-time, he'd give you the kinda hours that you'd have to quit. I've seen him do that before."

At that moment Mirta called out, "Lissette, can you please come here for a minute?" And Lissette went to the front counter, while I tried to think of another solution.

When Lissette came back, she said, "See that. One of your regulars just came up to the counter and said she thought she saw you back here and could you come out and give her a consultation. I told her you were off today and you were only stopping by for a few minutes. Carlos, that happens a lot when you're not here. People ask for you, and Valentino can't stand it. If he knows about this gig with Shirlena Day, I'm pretty sure he will find a way to make you kiss FeatureFace good-bye, hon."

"So what do you suggest I do, Lissette? Call Shirlena and tell her, 'I'm sorry. I can't come and take the opportunity of a lifetime because I'm scared my boss will be jealous and try to fire me?"

"It's the truth, isn't it?" she squealed.

Both of us stood at the back counter looking at the floor as if we expected an answer to spell itself out on the carpet any second.

"I think . . ." Lissette said. "I think you have to take this opportunity. And maybe you have to take a risk at the same time."

"What does that mean?" I asked her, not really sure I was ready for what she had to say.

"I think you should see if there are enough samples to take what you need. That way you won't be taking actual stock. If there are enough, then you take them and you go do Shirlena's makeup. If she likes it, you tell her to call Valentino and place a huge order, or have her show call and it won't matter. Valentino can take credit for the big sale, which you know he will, and if he gets the commission on it, he won't care how he got it. But in the meantime Shirlena will get to see how good you are!" Lissette took a deep breath and ran her hands over her breasts like they were the exclamation points to her sentence.

"I don't know," I said.

"What do you mean, you don't know? You gonna pass this up?"

"No, but I never pictured me taking anything without Valentino knowing. I just think no matter what happens, he'll try to have me sent to Rikers, and trust me, I won't be trying to be no makeup artist there in my cell."

"No, honey, you can set up a nice little table in the social hall or the mess hall or wherever it is all the inmates get together and socialize." Lissette started laughing so hard, her liner started to run.

"That's just hysterical," I whined. "Now could you please be serious and tell me what to do."

"Exactly what I said." Lissette suddenly stopped laughing. "You don't have any choice. You will never, ever get Valentino's permission, so you can either call Shirlena Day right now and make your apologies and tell her you can't come, or start packing makeup."

So I thought about it for a minute or two, and then I went to the drawer to get the samples. It took me less than three seconds to see that I'd never have enough. Crap! I knew I'd have to take the actual products to make sure I had what I needed. I took a deep breath and got a plastic shopping bag.

I think I was probably praying as I was packing. It certainly felt like stealing to me. Yes, I was using it for a customer. But no, the customer wasn't paying before the makeup left the store. Wait—

I pulled out my cell phone. Lissette said, "Are you really gonna call Valentino anyway? I'm telling you, it's a mistake."

"Shhhh." I told Lissette. When I heard Shirlena's voice message I was disappointed, but I went ahead anyway. "Hi, Shirlena. This is Carlos. I'm here at Macy's and I'm packing everything up, and I wanted to ask you, if we—or if *you* like the way things look after I do your makeup for the show, can I make a record of what we use and the producers of your show can buy it? So then, in a way, it would be like I'm doing a consultation at the studio with our products, and then, just like you'd do in the store, you'd purchase them. Except it wouldn't be you, it would be the producers of your show." I was babbling, but I managed to get it out. It was a way for me to feel that I wasn't about to steal a couple hundred dollars' worth of makeup. "When you get this message, could you call me right away? I'm bringing everything we need anyway, so you don't have to worry."

No, only *I* had to worry that she wouldn't get the message, and I'd think everything was all right until I'd used all the makeup on Monday and she told me, "No, I never agreed to any such thing." Could that actually happen? Yes, but it wouldn't. I had to have faith.

I clicked off and kept loading the bag with makeup. Lissette said, "I think that was pure genius, Carlos. I really do."

And I said, "Thanks. Let's hope she calls. I really don't wanna be trying to manage that makeup counter for the inmates at Rikers Island."

Chapter 28

I was on my way out of the store when my phone rang. I didn't even check to see who was calling. I answered hoping that before I got out of the store, Shirlena would have told me she'd gladly pay for whatever FeatureFace products I took from the store to use on her.

So it was a shock when I said "Hi" and a strange man's voice said "Hey" back.

"I'm sorry, who is this?" *Great,* I thought. *It's stupid Christian, Shirlena's makeup artist, calling to make my life more complicated.*

But it wasn't. "Hey, you don't know who this is?" And by then I did.

"Gleason?"

"Yeah, how are ya?"

I kept moving out of the store onto Seventh Avenue. "I'm okay. What'samatter?"

I heard a snorty laugh. "Nothing's the matter. I wanted to ask you something."

I frowned. The last time I'd spent more than a few minutes with him was at his opening. He'd acted like two different people, and worse than that, within minutes after I'd given him a bouquet of roses, he'd given it to some girl I'd never seen or heard about before. Or at least that's what it looked like. So, on the way home, Angie gave me a pep talk. She told me how, even though she didn't know where or when exactly, some guy twice as good-looking and twice as talented as Gleason would fall deeply in love with me. And he wouldn't send out a hundred mixed messages. And that night I told myself to bury my infatuation with him, so that when I'd seen him at school after that, I almost didn't mind him patting me on the shoulder or the back and giving me his I'd-love-to-stop-and-chat-but-I'm-too-busy-being-a-rock-star vibe. I'd gotten to the point where I barely looked up. Not that my eyes didn't follow him down the hallway till he completely disappeared, but he never knew it.

So where was this "I wanted to ask you something" coming from?

"Sure, Gleason, what can I do for you?" I was purposely sounding like I was still in the store behind the counter, except that I didn't even talk to clients like that.

"Do you have some time that we could . . . um . . . hang out?"

Hang out? If it had been any time before his opening, *before* I saw him kissing Gabs Cranberryhead holding *my* bouquet of roses, I would have told him the next six months were free. But not now.

"Actually, I'm superbusy right now. At least today and tomorrow."

"Oh. I was thinking since it was Sunday, maybe you weren't so . . . I don't know. . . . So you're busy all day, huh?"

"Kind of. What do you want to talk about? Is it important?"

"It's sort of important. But I guess it can wait," he said. "You say you're busy tomorrow, huh?" He sounded disappointed. I thought about how good he'd been to me when we were working on my pictures, the same pictures that helped get me my job at FeatureFace to begin with.

"Yeah, Gleason, tomorrow is very busy. I have school like you do, and then I have a job to do Monday night." God, it felt good to call it a job! "Could we talk on Tuesday? Or do you want to try to meet in school tomorrow?"

"No, not in school. Tuesday's cool. No problem."

"Are you sure?"

"Yeah, I'm sure."

"Should we pick a place now or do you want to figure it out tomorrow? Or you can text me if for some reason we don't see each other."

"Yeah," Gleason said. "I'll speak to ya or text ya tomorrow."

This is hysterical. Gleason Kraft is going to contact me tomorrow to meet on Tuesday after I told him I was too busy today and tomorrow. Insane. Am I conscious?

I clicked off and ran for the subway, picturing Gleason Kraft. *Beyond beautiful Gleason Kraft. Maybe he wants to do more pictures. Would I do them? Sure. I'd probably do anything for Gleason Kraft. Even if he does have an insufferable girlfriend with cranberry dyed hair.*

Chapter 29

Monday at school Gleason gave me the usual pat on the shoulder and a smile. It was as though he'd never called. Yeah, he was with his friends, which he always was. And, yeah, he was on the run, which he always was. But it was as though we hadn't made a date just hours before to meet the next day.

I didn't let it weird me out, though. I had only one thing on my mind—my date with Shirlena Day that night. After school I would go to the day care center. Being around the kids always helped me to focus when I had something important coming up. The thing about kids is that you have to pay attention right there and then. It's not about the future or the past—it's about "I'm hungry," "I'm wet," "I'm sleepy," and that means right now. So it always helped me to figure out how to cope with stuff in the moment, not before or after.

When I left the center, I'd go home, change, grab my makeup bag, and take the subway uptown to the studio. It was midtown and, from the address, I knew it was way over on Eleventh Avenue. That meant I'd have to make sure to give myself enough time for a long walk after I got off the subway. I paced myself at school, which means I had this look on my face in class that said, *I'm listening, I really am. You don't even have to call on me. Just keep teaching and know that I'm listening.* And, of course, I wasn't hearing much of what anybody said.

When I was standing at my locker, staring into it as though the books were going to fly out and into my arms magically, Angie said to me, "You may as well have stayed home. You're not here, that's for sure."

"And what would I have done at home? Watch the YouTube clips of Shirlena on *Smokin' Friday Nights* for the thousandth time? No, I'm trying to have as normal a day as possible. I'm trying to stay focused and keep projecting positive energy."

"Yeah, well, if walking through the halls in a trance with a smile on your face like you're competing for a beauty pageant is your idea of projecting positive energy, then I guess you're doing a great job! The only time I saw you snap out of it was when Gleason Kraft swatted you on the shoulder, and then you probably had more focused energy than I've seen out of you all day."

"By the way," I told her hurriedly, "I got a call from him. He wants to meet me to talk about something, and he says it's important. What do you think *that's* about?"

Angie looked worried. "I don't know, honey, but I really don't want you to let him make you nuts."

I laughed. "You mean break my heart?"

Angie shrugged. "Something like that."

"Listen," I told her, "I've got to run. I'll be late for class and I'm leaving right after that for the day care center. Give me a kiss for good luck tonight!"

Angie leaned over and gave me an air kiss, which was great, because she had some pretty nasty-looking crumbs on her lips from this cruller she was scarfing down.

When I got to the center, things were so crazy they weren't all that pleased that I was only going to be there for an hour. But the thing was, I'm so good with kids and the kids love me so much that even an hour is better than me calling in. And besides, I'm a hard worker.

Forget about staying in the moment, though. It usually worked, but not today. But it didn't matter too much if I was a little preoccupied. It wasn't like I was gonna drop one of the kids or something. I'd play with Serene, or change Tujami's diaper, or help Chrystal drink her juice, and the whole time I'd be applying makeup to Shirlena's face in my mind. But with kids, if you love them, they feel it, and unless you're *totally* distracted and pouring juice down the front of them, you can still be caring and they appreciate it and give you love back. On the other hand, you can give supposedly mature people *all* your attention and they *still* don't appreciate it.

By the time I left, I was tingling with excitement. I still had to go home and get dressed—there was no way I was setting foot in a major television studio without looking fabu-fierce! Besides my outfit, I'd decided my hair was long enough to put back in a ponytail—and not one of those pitiful ones that looks like a growth on your neck either. Mine would be shiny and what I call Puerto Rican–Dominican–Indian black. It would be substantial-looking, like there was lots more hair under there, even though there wasn't.

In other words I was going to give them, *I'm in the industry and I'm a pro, so don't even think about trying to mess with me!* Not that Shirlena would. I just wanted to tell anybody else who saw how young I was and doubted my talent to keep their distance!

On the way home to change, Ma called. If she'd known about me going to Metro Studios to do Shirlena's makeup, I'd have thought she was calling to wish me good luck. But because she was so preoccupied with Rosalia, I hadn't told her anything about it. I didn't want to announce my good news while she was so upset. I didn't tell Rosalia, either, so nobody in my family knew.

"Hey, Ma," I answered rushing into our apartment building.

"You didn't see I tried to call you before? Why didn't you call me back?"

"I'm sorry, Ma. You know I always turn my phone off at work. And I just got out, so no, I didn't see it. What's the matter?"

"What's the matter? I keep thinking about this mess with Rosalia, and you said to let you have a chance to fix it, so I wanna know if you've done anything yet. I'm not gonna wait around till something else happens, Carlos."

I was running up the stairs, wishing I could have this conversation anytime but now. "I know it's important, Ma."

"So did you do anything? Did you see that piece of crap who's hurting your sister?"

"No, Ma, I haven't seen him yet. But you promised to let me handle it. And I will. But I still go to school and I still work and I'm sorry I didn't do it yet, but I will. Can you trust me, please!" Yeah, I was kinda worked up, but the whole thing was *beyond upsetting*. So much for the positivity I was trying to channel for the night.

"All right, Carlos. But I'm telling you right now, I'm not gonna see her hurt and listen to her lie about it and not do anything!"

"I know, Ma, and neither am I."

Then, of course, she hung up without a "good-bye" or "see ya later" or anything. What I wished for was, "Good luck tonight," or "I hope everything goes well for you," but I knew that wasn't possible. How could she say that if she didn't know what I was doing? And maybe it was selfish of me to want her to be thinking about me at all, under the circumstances.

The whole time I was at home getting dressed, I thought about my conversation with Ma about Rosalia and Danny, or "the piece of crap," as Ma had started referring to him.

I didn't even try to focus on the night ahead of me. I got dressed and did my hair and packed my bag and even checked myself in the mirror fifty times, all the while hearing Ma's voice in my head. "I'm not gonna see her hurt and listen to her lie about it and not do anything!"

It's not like I wasn't going to do anything about it. I just didn't know what. Or how. Or when. Did that make me an uncaring brother? I wasn't sure. And that made me ashamed. I had to do something. Fast.

Chapter 30

M etro Studios was so far west, I expected to see covered wagons. I'm not even sure I'd ever been that far
over on the west side of the city. My feet were telling me
that maybe I should have worn my UGGs and changed into
my boots with the high heels once I got to the studio, but,
like I said, I wasn't really concentrating when I was getting
dressed.

In fact, I was so paranoid that I'd forgotten something,
I must have checked my makeup bag six times between the
apartment and the studio door. When I got about a block
away, I started to shake. I laughed at myself. Even though I
was a nervous wreck, I was excited. I was a half hour early. It
was five o'clock, and Shirlena said she didn't need me until
five thirty, but since when was being early a bad thing? I
figured I'd set up if I could and be ready to work as soon as
Shirlena needed me.

Getting into the studio was easier than I'd expected.
Shirlena had left my name on a list, and I showed my picture
ID from Macy's to the guard. After he checked my name,
I signed in and took the elevator up to the studio. For a
second I had a flash of what it might be like to come there

on a regular basis. I'd know the guard and say, "Hi, Harry," or George or Enrique and go on up to Metro to work with Shirlena. Maybe someday. But today I had to be genius—*beyond genius!*

The *Smokin' Friday Nights* studio was on the third floor. When I got off the elevator, it looked like I'd walked into a huge auditorium with bleachers set up in it. It was pretty dark, and there were men setting up stage lights at the front. When one of the few women passed by me, I asked like Shirlena had told me to, "Do you know where Shirlena Day's dressing room is, please?"

"Yeah. All the dressing rooms are back there down the hallway." She pointed. "And Shirlena's is about third or fourth on the right, I think."

I walked in the dark in the direction that she'd pointed in, and when I got to the area where the dressing rooms were, I stopped and looked back at the bleachers where the audience would be. *Yep, I'm really here.*

I walked down the hallway, expecting to see stars on the dressing room doors, I guess, but there weren't any. Instead there were either old, fun movie posters or posters of CD covers on them. One had a *Star Wars* poster on it and another had a *Saturday Night Fever* poster on it. When I got to the third dressing room on the right, it had an old Aretha Franklin album cover on it, and I guessed it was Shirlena's, but I wasn't completely sure. People were passing me in the narrow hallway, and I didn't want to ask anyone again. I was trying to look like I knew where I was going, but eventually, after I'd gone up and down the hall a couple of times, I saw a guy with a couple of dresses on a clothes rack use a key to get into the dressing room with the Aretha Franklin cover on it. I waited until he came out.

"Excuse me. I was looking for Shirlena Day's dressing room. Is that it?"

"That's it, but nobody's home," the guy told me. "She'll probably be here in maybe a half hour."

"Thanks." I watched him move down the hallway, stopping in a couple of other dressing rooms, dropping off what were probably costumes. I was trying to figure out where to wait. I didn't want to go back downstairs and stand outside. But what would I do for a half hour? There wasn't any place for me to even sit that I knew of.

I ran toward the last dressing room I'd seen the guy go into. When he came out, I said, "I was supposed to meet Shirlena here, but I'm early. Do you know if there's anywhere I could wait?"

"You could go to the cafeteria. Ya just keep going this way and turn to the left. You'll see it."

"Thanks a lot," I told him. As I was walking away, he yelled to me, "Nice boots!"

"Thanks!" I practically runway-walked down the rest of the hall.

When I got to what the guy had called the cafeteria, I was expecting to see what we had at school. But this was a pretty small room that looked like a waiting room with chairs and leather couches and a little area where a man stood behind a counter and heated food in a microwave for people. Nobody seemed to be paying for anything, except when they used the vending machines. I took out some quarters and got a Diet Coke.

I opened my bag and started going through it, checking what I'd brought against my list for the ninetieth time. After about fifteen minutes I heard two people speaking and I looked up. There was Adam Lambert in this jumpsuit that was so tight I honestly believe somebody must have sewn him into it. Then it hit me. He must have been the musical guest star for the week. I hadn't even thought about any part of the show other than Shirlena's. Maybe I'd get to see Adam Lambert perform too. That would be juicy.

He and the guy he was with went to the vending machine and bought sodas. On his way out, I'd like to believe Adam glanced at me and we smiled at each other. But it might have been my imagination. I gotta admit, I'd already started to feel that the whole thing was a little supernatural, so who knows? But that's how I'll remember it anyway.

At twenty after five I couldn't sit there any longer. I got up and went back down the hall to Shirlena's dressing room. The door was partially open, and I could hear her in there singing. I knocked and called in at the same time, "Shirlena?"

She opened the door smiling. "I was just going to come look for you. There was a rumor there was a man looking for me, and I know where my seventeen boyfriends are, so I thought it must be you. Did you get here early?"

"A little, but I went into the cafeteria and had a soda."

"Sorry if I kept you waiting. I thought you might show up a couple of minutes early, but didn't I say five thirty?"

"Oh, you did. I guess I just wanted to make sure I got here on time, since I didn't know exactly where I was going."

Shirlena smiled. "I'm so used to Christian sauntering

in here late. Usually I start doing my own makeup and he comes in, if I'm lucky, just in time to do Michelle O."

Exactly as Shirlena was saying it, a voice behind us snapped, "Well, he's here on time tonight."

I knew it had to be Christian. He was very, very blond with superlong black eyelashes and huge blue eyes. He looked like he spent most of his time either working out or at a tanning center, or maybe someplace where he could do both at the same time. His arms and legs were gimungous, and his skin was this deep, dark beige color. Believe me, I come from a whole race of brown-colored people in all different shades of it, and none of us look the color that Christian was. It was kind of a cocoa with some orange mixed in. Very strange.

"I didn't know whether you were coming in or not, Christian," Shirlena said to him, sitting on a tiny couch against the dressing room wall.

"Why wouldn't I come? We're shooting tonight, aren't we?" Christian's tone was definitely *not* friendly.

And apparently Shirlena was *not* having it. "Carlos, would you mind waiting outside for a moment? I would like to speak to Christian in private."

"Of course," I said, and eased by *the blond hulk* to get outside the dressing room, pulling the door shut behind me.

It was barely closed before I heard, "I can't believe you. How dare you come in here speaking to me like that? And in front of a complete stranger? Not that it matters. You shouldn't be speaking to me like that at all. What exactly is your problem, Christian?"

"I don't have any problem, Shirlena. I thought maybe

you had a problem. First there are all these rumors going around about how unhappy you are with me because you think I have a bad attitude—"

"You don't have to hear rumors, Christian. I've told you to your face. Your attitude is lousy. I told you that the damn makeup was making me break out, and instead of you trying to figure out how we could solve the problem, you gave me this song and dance about how makeup was makeup and there was nothing you could do about it and maybe I should see a skin specialist. And all I had to do—which is what I expected you to do—was do some research and see if maybe there was something else that we could use that would work and not make me look like my face was exploding. And tonight you come in here with an attitude worse than ever—"

"How can you say I have an attitude when I came in on time?"

"That's not a favor, Christian. That's your job!"

"Well, how do I know I even have a job if I come in and that little boy is in here with his little makeup bag all ready to go?"

"You know I asked you to work with him after he agreed to help you find something—"

"I don't need an assistant, Shirlena! And if I did, it seems to me I should be the one to hire him, not you!"

"You know what? That's it! I came in here to work tonight, and you came in here to cause trouble, and I can't work with you tonight and I don't think I want to work with you again. So could you please leave!"

"*Excuse* me?"

"You heard me, Christian. I want you out of here. Now!"

I was shocked, but not so shocked that I didn't move as quickly as I could down the hall and away from Shirlena's door. I didn't make it that far. When Christian came out, I couldn't help but watch him. He slammed the door and walked past me without looking at me, but I could feel his energy.

I didn't know what to do next, so I stayed outside the dressing room. Seconds later Shirlena opened the door. "I'm sorry you had to hear that, and I'm sure you did. Are you all right?"

"Me?" I answered. "I'm fine. How are *you* doing?"

Shirlena laughed. "Are you kidding?" Then she motioned for me to come in. When I got inside, she closed the door. "I hate to say it, but I'm relieved. I hate bad vibes. They make it impossible to do good work. And that's what we're here to do—work."

"Yes," I said energetically. But I was more shook up than I wanted her to know. I never expected to witness anything like that. I thought the whole thing would be one big joy-filled adventure. But it definitely hadn't started out that way.

"Carlos, I've seen what you do, and I think you're great. The question is, do you think you can handle this tonight? I asked the other makeup people, and they really don't have time to supervise you. If you don't think you can do it, one of them will just take over for the night. I mean, we have a little time for you to try stuff out, and I know all the steps, so I'm not panicking or anything. But what do you think? Do you want to give it a try?"

I thought maybe I was back in the big joy-filled adventure, that's what I thought. "Absolutely," I told her. "No problem at all!"

Shirlena told me, "We do a basic look for all the skits, and then you'll have about ten minutes to freshen it up when I change to do Michelle O."

"I know I can do it," I told her.

There was a big outline of Shirlena's face on her dressing room mirror, and she'd written down all of the steps so she could do them herself in an emergency. Once I knew what products Christian used, it was simple to substitute what I'd already guessed would work.

When I'd finished, Shirlena took a long look in the mirror. I knew what I was seeing. But it was what she thought that counted.

"Fabulous!" Shirlena told me. "And so far, no itching!"

Shirlena told me I could come out into the audience for the first part of the show, which she thought would be pretty special since I'd never been in a TV audience before. Even if I had, nothing could have compared with *Smokin' Friday Nights*. It was a "can't-miss" for a lot of people in the country, so having anything to do with it—especially as a makeup artist—was thrilling. I was determined not to let her down.

She'd told me that after a sketch about people in a supermarket, she would come offstage and I should be ready to help her do the ten-minute change into Michelle O. She gave me the key to her dressing room so I could get in.

What she hadn't thought of was that it would be impossible for me to get from the audience to the dressing room once the show had started. So I decided to watch the show on a monitor in her dressing room. That would give me more time to get ready for her anyway.

Sitting in her dressing room, I'd look from the monitor to the hanger where her Michelle O dress was, and then to the wig stand, remembering her saying, "Once I've got the wig on, the incredible actress that I am takes over." I'd laid out all the makeup, and I felt pretty confident. By the time the supermarket sketch started, I felt like I'd been doing the whole thing for years.

A few minutes later I heard a lot of applause coming from the studio, and Shirlena swept in like a thunderstorm. "Hey, Mr. Carlos! Are we ready?"

I went into automatic. "We sure are."

"Great. First I get dressed. Then you can put the bib on me and we have ten minutes for me to put the wig on and you to freshen me up!"

We were actually finished ahead of time. I realized I was holding my breath. Lisa, the head makeup woman, came in and took a look at what I'd done.

"Well, if it isn't the first lady herself!" And then, in a Wendy Williams drawl, she asked Michelle O, "How you doin'?"

Shirlena laughed, and I tried, but I swear the muscles in my face weren't working. All I could do was stare at Shirlena and think that I'd been a part of it.

The show hairstylist bounced in and gave the wig a few teases and pats, and Shirlena was up on her feet and heading for the door. She was almost gone when she turned around and rushed toward me. She had so much energy, I almost ducked. But she kissed me on the cheek and said, "Thank you, Carlos. You did great!" And then she ran out into the hallway. When I went to the door, there were three other cast members who were playing Secret Service men running alongside her, and I thought, *Damn, Carlos. You really did do great.*

I sat on her little dressing room couch and stared around me. I was a high school student who had just done Shirlena Day's makeup for a TV show. I was one step closer to going from a kid wannabe to Carrlos Duarte, a famous makeup artist. I looked up on the monitor and saw Shirlena's close-up as Michelle O. OMG! OMG! OMG! How could I get about seventy-five gazillion copies of this?

And that's when the call came.

He'd only called me a couple of times before. Every time I knew that it was him, I took a deep breath before I answered.

"Hello?" I said quietly.

"What would make you think you could steal hundreds of dollars' worth of makeup from FeatureFace Cosmetics and get away with it?"

"I don't know what you're talking about, Valentino." My voice was shaking. Of course I knew what he was talking about. It was my worst nightmare.

I'd left the message for Shirlena about buying all of the makeup, but we hadn't had time to talk about it, and now Valentino was already calling it stealing.

"Valentino, I just used the makeup on Shirlena Day for *Smokin' Friday Nights.* I'm sure she's going to buy it."

"But she didn't buy it! Customers buy makeup *before* they leave the store, or they pay for it and it's sent to them. Company employees don't steal the makeup and then claim the customer bought it and will pay for it when she feels like it."

"But she *will* pay for it—"

"Forget it, Carlos. You'll never work in this industry again! So I hope whatever you think you're doing with Shirlena Day works out, because when we press charges, you're going to need all the money you can get." And then he was gone.

I put my phone on Shirlena's little dressing room couch and realized I was trembling again. I wasn't afraid. I was angry. I was angry that I was stupid enough to take the makeup out of the store and put myself in this position, and I was angry that Valentino was so jealous of me that he was twisting something like this to make it look like I was a thief, when all I was really trying to do was . . . Was what? I suppose it was to make myself look better, and it *was* true that I hadn't bought the makeup, so yes, it was stealing, wasn't it? And what if they did press charges? Could I go to jail? No, I was too young. Wasn't I? But they could still send me to some kind of prison *somewhere*. God. Why was I so stupid?

I waited for Shirlena to come offstage from doing the Michelle O sketch. She came in laughing. "It was super! Do you think it had anything to do with the makeup?"

"I don't know," I said quietly.

"Well, I do," she said. "Honey, I have to change really quickly for the next sketch. Would you mind standing outside for just a second?"

"No, of course not," I told her, and got out of the dressing room as quickly as I could. I had to talk to her. I'd wait until after the show.

When she came rushing out, she said, "This is the last one. Wait for me. We gotta figure out how you get paid."

I hadn't even thought about getting paid. I'd been so crazy to do it, I would have done it three nights in a row before it hit me that people probably got paid a lot of money to do what I was doing. Didn't they? They had to be making more than what I made at Macy's working for FeatureFace, even when they sent me out for a "special store appearance." Maybe what I'd get paid would at least cover what I'd taken from the store. That way, Valentino wouldn't press charges and the worst that could happen is that I'd get fired.

"You'll never work in this industry again." I was sure if he had anything to do with it, I wouldn't. And to have a reputation as a thief on top of that? I could feel tears starting to cloud my eyes.

I'd talk to Shirlena. I'd remind her about the message and ask her if she'd call Valentino and tell him what the makeup was for. Then, even if she or the show didn't buy the makeup, maybe FeatureFace wouldn't think of what I'd done as theft, just as stupidity.

When Shirlena came back into the dressing room, I bombarded her. I didn't want to, but I had to.

"Shirlena, I have to talk to you and it's really important."

Shirlena stared at me. "I can't believe you look like that. You just had a real success here! You should be proud of yourself."

"I am. It's just that . . ."

"It's just that what?"

"Shirlena, did you get my message about the makeup?"

"Your message about the—oh, yes! I did. I forgot! I can write you out a check for it and have the studio reimburse me. And please get some more. Unless I break out tomorrow like I've been doing, I want to stock up on this! And the reason I think we're good is because by now, usually

with the other stuff, I'm already starting to itch and swell."
Shirlena went to her purse and pulled out her checkbook.
"How much was it?"

I told her I had to figure it out and I'd get back to her,
but that wasn't the point.

"No? What is the point?"

"The point is, I took it out of the store before it was paid
for, and now my boss, Valentino, is calling it theft and I'm
probably going to get fired."

"You're kidding."

"I wish."

"I'll call him. That's all. I'll call him and tell him I told
you I needed it and I was going to cover it. And I will."

"Thank you, Shirlena. I appreciate it."

"Then why do you still look like you've been trapped in
a morgue?"

"Oh, no. I don't mean to. I really do appreciate it." And
I gave her a big fake grin.

Shirlena sat at her mirror and started to take off her
makeup. It made me sad, as though it was symbolic or something. What I didn't want to tell her was that I was pretty
sure no matter what she said, Valentino was still going to
use it as an excuse to fire me. Like he said, Shirlena was *his*
customer. And I'd stolen her, too. Even if she didn't know it.
No, I was pretty sure I'd have to pay for what I'd done. Even
if he didn't press charges, I could definitely kiss my career
with FeatureFace good-bye.

chapter 32

Tuesday morning I wanted to wake up anyplace other than New York City. With a different name, different everything. Maybe it's because everything I wanted Carrlos Duarte to be was going to be ruined with FeatureFace firing me for stealing.

I wanted to think about what a success I'd had last night. Everything with Shirlena had been *beyond brilliant*, even though it had gotten off to a rocky start. For the next ten years I wanted to work with Shirlena on *Smokin' Friday Nights* and whatever else she wanted me to do. The feeling was incredible. I hadn't even graduated high school and I had done Shirlena Day's makeup on a superpopular TV show.

And the reality was, I couldn't tell my mother, because she wouldn't be interested. Because my sister was getting beaten up by her boyfriend, and all Ma could think about was murdering him. And I couldn't really consider it a success anyway, because I'd used makeup I'd stolen from the company, even though I didn't consider it stealing when I did it. And now I was going to get fired and I'd probably never get work in the makeup industry again. Nobody hires thieves, especially in department stores.

Of course there was the fantasy that Shirlena would hire me. I'd done a damn good job, and she knew it. But I was a high school student. How could she convince the producers of *Smokin' Friday Nights* to hire a kid who wasn't out of high school? No, my one night of fame and glamour was over. Now I wouldn't even be able to get a job in a department store.

I dragged myself to school. Angie knew from a glance that I had lots to fill her in on. But I couldn't even begin. With Angie and me, it's either all the details or nothing. I told her, "I can't even begin to talk about it. All I can ask you is, if I was put in jail, would you come and visit?"

She said, "With a carrot cake every weekend." Then we kissed each other's cheeks and hugged. She whined, "Carlos!"

But I said, "I told you. Don't ask!"

I went to my locker, and there was a note stuck in it. I opened it and read:

> Hey Carlos dn't forget were suppozzed to meet. How abt. Tompkins Sq pk.? I'll giv u a call. Gleas

I don't know how I did it, but I *had* forgotten. Believe it or not, the last thing I wanted to do was meet Gleason Kraft, no matter how curious I'd been before or how crushed-out I was. Today was not the day. I felt like I was at a funeral for my life.

I decided that when I saw him in the hallway and he gave me one of his I'm-just-letting-you-know-I-see-you-but-I'm-not-going-to-stop-cause-I'm-with-my-cool-rocker-buddies pats on the shoulder, I was going to say really fast, "We're not meeting, Gleason. I can't do it today" and just let him deal with it.

The thing was, I didn't see him all day.

At the end of the day when I was in my last class, good old Music Appreciation, I got a call from him that I couldn't answer. When I got out of class, I saw that I had a voice mail.

"Hey, this is Gleas. I'll meet you in the park at the big circle after school at four. If you can't come, it's okay, but it's kind of important." Wonderful.

What was with this "Gleas" all of a sudden, and how could I not show up if he said it was important?

On the way to the park I decided to give the store a call to see if I could speak to Lissette. Maybe she could tell if Valentino was still in the mood to press charges against me, or at least if Shirlena had called.

"FeatureFace Cosmetics, Lissette speaking. How may I help you?"

"Lissette, it's Carlos. Can you talk, or is Valentino there?"

"I'm sorry, ma'am. But I'd be happy to call you later and let you know, if you'd like."

That meant he was there and she couldn't talk. "Do you know if Shirlena called?" I asked her.

"No, I'm sorry. But I'm hoping we get it in soon." Damn.

"Okay. Thanks, Lissette. Please call me later and tell me what you can."

"I'll be sure and do that, ma'am."

Okay, so that probably meant that Valentino was busy trying to figure out what he was going to wear in court when they pressed charges against me.

• • •

As soon as I got inside the park, I saw Gleason from a distance. Considering it was winter, it was really warm, and there he was in a short leather jacket and bright red tight corduroy jeans. If I wasn't so depressed, I would have probably been more excited about just looking at him sitting there.

He waved to me as though he'd been waiting.

"Hey, Gleas," I called, half teasing. I had to ask him what was up with that. It was obnoxious-sounding.

"Thanks for coming," he said, and gave me this big spine-crunching hug. He kind of bounced up and down in place like a marionette and then he landed on the bench.

"What's so important?" I asked, sitting down beside him. Not as close as I used to imagine sitting next to him one day, but there we were.

Gleason looked down at his black and red Keds. "You know . . . how I was so excited for you to come to my opening?"

Well, he'd seemed excited about having a show. And then he'd ditched me and Angie to go hang out at the bar with Cranberryhead and gave her *my* roses. But I said simply, "I remember that you were excited to have a show. And who wouldn't be?"

"No, Carlos. I was excited because we'd worked on those photographs together and now they were huge and they were hanging in a gallery and I wanted to . . . uh . . . share it with you."

Maybe it was because I was preoccupied with the whole Valentino thing, I don't know, but Gleason Kraft was not having the same effect on me today that he usually had.

"No, Gleason, I didn't really get all that. I was glad to be invited, though." Then I did something way out of character for me, especially where Gleason was concerned. I said to him, "Gleason, you said this was important, so I'm here. But I have some stuff on my mind that's really upsetting and important, so do you want to tell me what you wanted to talk about?"

I could see he was surprised. I didn't mean to be rude at all. But I *was* being selfish. I needed to think. Or I needed to go to Macy's and plead my case. Or to call Shirlena and ask her if she'd had a chance to speak to Valentino. But I definitely didn't need to be sitting on a park bench with Gleason chitchatting about his opening, which had already happened and which he'd pretty much ignored me at.

"I'm sorry you're upset about something. Is there anything I can do?"

"No," I told him. "And I don't want you to think you can't talk to me about whatever it is . . ."

"I guess I'm kind of stalling, because I know how stupid this is going to sound, and you probably already know what I'm going to say."

And I did. Suddenly I did. I wasn't 100 percent sure. But I was 99.9 percent sure.

"I'm not good at guessing, Gleason. And I don't want to appear really stupid and embarrass myself. I'm not in the mood." I laughed. I didn't know where it came from.

"I . . . I was talking to Gabs—uh Gabrielle . . . you remember her, right?"

"Yeah, Gleason, I couldn't possibly forget Gabs." I didn't mean to sound so snarky, but I wanted him to get whatever it was *out* already.

"Well, she was saying how she thought maybe I should have a talk with you."

I stared at him for a second. "Yeah? About what?" Did I just say I was 99.9 percent sure what he was going to say? Well, in less than a minute I had no clue whatsoever. So much for my fabulous instincts. "We barely met each other, and then you went to the bar and that was the last I saw of you . . . and Gabs. What could she think you should have a talk with me about?"

"I've told her a lot about you."

It was like reading a mystery and wanting to skip to where you find out who the killer is. "You have? That's interesting. And?"

"So she knows how talented I think you are, and how much I owe you for asking me to do the model pictures in the first place."

"No, Gleason, you don't owe me anything. You took great pictures, and you got a show from them. The show part had nothing to do with me."

"Okay. But I'm still grateful." And then we sat there, with him looking at the ground and me knowing he didn't make an appointment to tell me again that he was thankful I'd asked him to take some pictures.

"Gleason, what did Gabs think you should talk to me about?"

Gleason scrunched his whole body up like it had suddenly gotten colder when it hadn't. "She said . . . She said she could tell from the way you . . . were . . . around me, and the roses and the . . . camera necklace thing . . . that you probably had a crush on me, and that if I wanted us to have a real friendship, I should probably speak to you and get it out in the open. So you wouldn't be . . . hurt."

The camera necklace thing?

"I may be sick," I said quietly.

I didn't feel the least bit sick. What I felt was embarrassed and furious—with myself, Gleason, and the lovely Gabs—but I didn't want to show it or say it.

"Why?" Gleason was the one who looked like he was about to heave. "I'm so sorry. Maybe I shouldn't have said anything, but she kept asking me if I'd talked to you yet. She said I owed it to you as a friend."

"That was very kind of her, Gleason. Very considerate." I wanted to jump up and run, but I knew if I didn't fix things now with him, it would be harder—much harder—later on.

"She always teases me and says how people probably think I'm gay. She calls me Gleason Gaybait. She says I'm the kind of guy gay guys always fall for."

"That's hysterical," I said, thinking it was way past time for me to be rid of Gleason "Gaybait" Used to Be a Crush Now Thought of as an Idiot. "Gaybait? Really, Gleason? Aren't you even embarrassed to repeat that?"

"I know it's stupid, but remember, *she* says it, not *me*."

"Gleason, it's late, and I have some important things to take care of. But before I leave"—and my voice was shaking because I was about to tell a very big lie—"I want you to know that I don't now and I never did have a crush on you. I didn't 'fall' for you like your girlfriend thought. I asked you to take some pictures. You did. They were good for you and they were good for me. I guess I made a big mistake by trying to show my appreciation. But in this case, Gabs's instincts are all wrong. I never thought about you as anything other than a kid in my school who takes excellent photographs." I got up dramatically from the bench, hoping like crazy that Gleason felt as foolish as I did. He jumped up also.

"I'm sorry if I said something wrong. I thought Gabs was crazy, but then she kept bringing it up—"

"Then maybe Gabs has the problem," I told him, smiling. "Like I said, I have some stuff to do, so I should probably head home."

Now, of course, Gleason looked like I'd hurt his feelings by denying I had a crush on him—*make up your mind, guy!* "Is there anything I can do to help you with whatever you're upset about?" he asked.

"No. I should just go now, that's all."

"I'll walk with you. Is that all right?"

"Sure. Thanks." What I was telling myself was, *This was surreal!*

But another voice inside me answered, *No, Carlos. It was too real!*

Gleason and I were almost at the park entrance when I saw him. Part of me wanted to turn around and go somewhere until I could figure out exactly what to do. And part of me wanted to run up to him before he realized what was going on and start punching him as hard as I could.

But I didn't do either. When Danny and his slimy friend from Burrito Take-Out Village looked up at me from their bench with smirks on their faces, everything stopped. And for a second I didn't see anything but them. I didn't hear anything. I felt like I was totally alone. There they were, and I knew I had to do something that would somehow make a difference.

chapter 33

"That your boyfriend, freak?" Danny called out to me. How ironic. I was used to it, but I expected Gleason would take off down the street and never look back.

I went right up to Danny. "You put your hands on my sister again, and I'll break your neck."

Danny got up from the bench and stood so close to me I could smell his foul liquored-up breath. Then he spat at me. It had barely splattered against my face when I saw his fist coming at me. As I fell back, I grabbed his shirt. I started to punch at him, throwing out my fists wildly just trying to reach his body. He smashed me between the eyes. I saw black spots. But I just kept swinging.

Then his friend came at me. I smelled both of them. I felt knuckles against my head like rocks. I closed my eyes, but I kept punching. It was like being thrown into the ocean. You just keep punching the water.

Somewhere, from what seemed like really far away, I heard Gleason's voice scream, "Stop! Stop!" And other people were yelling too, but it all sounded like it was in the distance.

One of the two guys hit me so hard on the head, it felt like it had to be more than his fist, but I don't know. What I do know is that it hurt so much, I started to sink. I lost my balance and started to fall in slow motion. My face skidded against the pavement and my leg twisted under me. It felt like it was broken.

Then I felt someone pull my arm. It hurt so badly, but I couldn't pull back. I was trying to get back up, but I didn't have the strength. Whoever it was let go of my arm and turned me over onto my back. I looked up at him. It was a cop.

"You all right?"

I couldn't say anything. It hurt too much. He put his hand under my head and lifted it off the ground. "Can you get up?"

I still couldn't answer right away. But I could see another cop holding on to Danny and his friend. They both stared at me, looking like they were hoping the cops would disappear so we could pick up where we left off. Closer to where I was, Gleason was also staring at me. His hands were covering his nose and mouth, and his face was covered in blood.

We looked at each other. I wanted to tell him I was sorry. It wasn't his fight. There was a small crowd standing there. The cop asked me again, "You think you can stand, or should we call an ambulance?"

"No," I heard myself say, but my ears were stopped up. "I can get up." The cop started to help me, and he said, "Somebody said these guys jumped you."

I looked at Danny and his friend. A woman called out,

"They did! You need me as a witness, you got it! Those boys were on their way out of the park, and then one of these kids said something to 'em and before you know it, they was beatin' the livin' daylights out of 'em."

"That true?" the cop said to me.

I didn't say anything.

"If they did, you gotta say something. If you wanna fill out a report, we'll take all o' yas to the precinct and you can fill out a report."

I looked at Danny. He wasn't afraid of anything. He was still sneering. I thought about Rosalia's face and the bruises and the nights I'd heard her in her room crying. And Ma saying to me, "Either you do something or I will."

"Yeah," I told the cop. "I want to do whatever I have to. They attacked me and my friend when we were leaving the park. And he also beat up my sister."

I told Gleason he didn't have to come with me, he didn't have to get involved. But he wanted to. The precinct was a few blocks away. I'd passed it dozens of times, but never thought I'd be inside.

I don't know what will happen with it all. The cops said they couldn't do anything about Rosalia, and then they said from the story the guys told, it wasn't clear if we were attacked or if it was a fight because I was mad about what "allegedly" happened to my sister. To hear Danny tell it, Rosalia was mad because he broke up with her. He claimed she told me lies and then me and Gleason attacked him and his friend because of what she'd said.

But you know what? I'm glad I filled out the papers and

I'm glad Danny heard me tell the cops what he'd done to Rosalia, because he knows he can't bully our family and get away with it. Because if it happens again, there will already be a record of it with the police. Seems to me that ought to mean *something*.

Gleason came home with me. At first he thought he had a broken nose, but it was only bleeding like crazy and swollen. A cop took a look at him at the police station and told him he should definitely have a doctor take a look at it, but that he didn't think it was broken. "That guy wasn't a doctor, Gleason. You should go to the emergency room," I told him.

But he said, "I just wanna make sure you get home first. You're a lot worse-looking than I am."

"Thanks, Gleason. That's reassuring," I said, and I would have laughed, except my whole face alternated between excruciating pain and no feeling at all. The cops actually drove us to my apartment building, which was a first for me, and I hope the last. They offered to take Gleason home too, but he insisted on coming to my apartment.

When we got upstairs, Ma was there. She went crazy. She took one look at me and wanted to take us *both* to the emergency room. I hadn't really seen myself, but when I did, I was *beyond horrified*. I don't really consider myself vain, but pleeeease! You should have seen me. It was scary.

I explained to her in detail what happened, and of course she was furious that now Danny had bruised not one but two of her kids. "Ma, let it go until we see what happens. At least I filled out the paperwork. If this jerk does anything else to anybody, his name is on file. Now the thing is trying to convince Ro that he's not a sane choice for a boyfriend."

Ma was working on me and Gleason at the same time. Wet washcloths, ice, Bacitracin ointment. "I'm not a surgeon, ya know," she said to Gleason. "I don't wanna keep doin' stuff to your nose and then have you find out it's broken. Your parents will sue me." Gleason laughed and promised they wouldn't.

I could tell she was really curious about him. She said to me in front of him, "You never mentioned Gleason to me. He's a good kid. And God knows, somebody who'll fight for you? That's more than a friend."

I told her loud and clear, "No, Ma, he's a good *friend*. Not *more* than a friend. A good *friend*." I hoped that satisfied Gleason. I didn't want him thinking he was "my hero" again, no matter what had happened in the park.

Ma even said she'd make dinner for us, but Gleason said he had to get home, which made sense considering the shape he was in.

When he left, I went out to the hall to talk to him for a minute. I would have gone downstairs except it hurt too much, and Ma said if she heard me on the stairs, she'd come get me and drag me back inside.

But I wanted to tell him thank you. And that I knew he didn't have to help me out there, especially since just before he'd gotten beaten up, he'd been trying to make his big disclaimer. He and I knew part of the reason for the fight was Rosalia, but part of it was because the pig brothers thought we were gay, and that was enough to beat on us.

"I'm not gonna stay out here long," I told him in the hallway. "I don't wanna scare my mother, but I feel like I'm *beyond dead*. So I'm gonna go in and go to bed. But I just wanna say I'm sooo sorry you got hurt, and thanks for not leaving me there."

"I wouldn't," Gleason said. "I haven't been in a freakin' fight since I was in fifth grade, but I wouldn't have left you there."

As he went down the stairs, I yelled to him, "Think about going to a doctor, just in case your nose is broken!"

And he yelled back up, "Sometimes guys with broken noses look really hot!"

Inside our apartment Ma was cleaning up the little emergency room she'd created. She said, "I didn't tell you to get yourself killed, Carlos. It's bad enough the guy was beatin' on your sister. I don't want him to kill the whole family."

"I didn't think about it, Ma. I guess I just kinda went crazy."

"Well, don't go so crazy that you get hurt. You're gonna be famous. You can't afford to get all scarred up."

I laughed. "I was bein' *manly*."

"I know," Ma laughed back. "Next time don't try so hard."

When I got into bed about twenty minutes later, I checked my phone for messages. Nothing. Nada. I decided that no matter what I felt like, I was skipping school the next day and going to Macy's. I was going to the FeatureFace counter and facing the Valentino dragon.

chapter 35

I looked as good as I could, considering. I put on my Gucci dark glasses—the biggest I owned—to cover as much of the bruising as possible. Classic oxford black linen shirt, tapered dress pants, and Florsheims. I looked like a fashionable priest going to beg for mercy. Or at least to try to clear my name.

A few feet from the counter, I saw Craig Denton. The same man who was practically responsible for hiring me. I turned around and went directly to the men's room. All I could think of was that Valentino had called him to come from the main offices and talk about the scandal: HIGH SCHOOL EMPLOYEE EMBEZZLES SEVERAL HUNDRED DOLLARS OF MERCHANDISE! WALKS OUT OF THE STORE WITH IT IN THE MIDDLE OF THE DAY!

I was hyperventilating. I'd pictured trying to calm a screaming Valentino, but I'd never pictured Valentino smirking over Craig Denton's shoulder as they waited for me to be arrested and dragged through the store in handcuffs.

Well, if that's the way it was going to be, then, okay. It was better than the cops coming to school to arrest me or to the apartment and having all the neighbors see. Poor Ma.

Carlos! Caaaarrrrllllooos! Get yourself together! I stopped daydreaming and came out of the stall. I washed my hands, waited until two other people left the bathroom, and looked at myself without my dark glasses on. What a horrible way to get arrested.

I slowly opened the door and walked what felt like five miles toward the counter. Lissette was there, waiting on a customer. She looked at me like I was arriving for my appointment with the electric chair. I mouthed "Hi" but nothing came out.

In a second and a half, Craig came out, followed by Valentino.

"Mr. Duarte. We were just talking about you." He stared at my face. "What on earth happened to you?"

I was shaking. How long did I have before he turned to Valentino and barked, "Call security! Immediately!"

"I fell," I told him, and I immediately thought of Rosalia's lies. I didn't know what else to say, and what difference did it make to him anyway? After he fired me, who cared what my face looked like if it wasn't going to be three inches away from customers' while I made them up?

Valentino was standing there looking like Mr. Frosty. Besides whatever else he thought about me, I don't imagine he had much of a stomach for bad bruises surrounded by dried blood, even half hidden under dark glasses.

"Val, did you say there was a place where we could meet privately with Mr. Duarte?"

Okay, so Craig Denton was calling me Mr. Duarte, as though it may as well have been "the defendant," and I was sure whatever room they were taking me to would have at least one detective in it, and probably a cop with a set of handcuffs just right for my pudgy little wrists.

I took one last look at Lissette as Valentino led us to the elevator. She looked like whatever I was headed for was happening to her. I guess she really liked me, I thought sadly.

We went up to the twelfth floor, where the human resources offices were. When we passed the tenth floor, where Angie worked in the Linens department, I tried to picture her saying a prayer for me, even if she wasn't working that day.

Valentino led us into what looked more like a conference room. There was a long table with chairs around it. He still hadn't said anything to me. I guessed he was about as happy as a shark in a pool full of fat people who were bleeding and couldn't swim.

Craig Denton told me, "Sit down, Carlos." I was grateful for the "Carlos" and that his tone sounded gentler. I sat, and so did they. Except they were across from me on the other side, like we were already in court.

"Let me get right to the point. Apparently you've done something pretty stupid."

I breathed in deeply, and kept looking at him.

"You could, as I understand it, be arrested for stealing from this company."

There was a second of silence before he asked, "Is that correct, Carlos?"

"I was hoping it would be considered borrowing stuff I needed until the customer could pay for it."

Valentino snorted.

"I mean, I was hoping that the customer was going to buy it and then it wouldn't be considered stealing."

Valentino finally said something. "The point is, the merchandise was carried out of the store—you carried it out of the store without paying for it. Isn't that right?"

"Yes," I said quietly.

"And that constitutes *theft*," Valentino said. It was true, but it was also true I could hear that Valentino was enjoying himself.

"And did you come back today to steal *more* merchandise?"

"Of course not. I mean, no, I didn't. I came back to talk to you about what happened."

"Carlos, you're a smart guy. With a lot of ambition," Craig said to me. "Don't you get that this could destroy any chance you might have at success in this business?"

"Yes, I do. Like you said, it was stupid. I wasn't thinking. I didn't mean to do anything criminal. I'm sorry."

Right on cue Valentino snorted again. Disgust was all over his face. He looked like he could smell me from where he was sitting across the table.

"The only thing that saved you in this mess was the deal we made with *SFN*, thanks to Shirlena Day," Craig said. "We could still fire you and take you to court if we wanted to. But I've decided to call what you did damned poor judgment instead of a criminal act. Shirlena called raving about what a genius job you did with her makeup for the show, and she said her producers were going to buy lots of everything you used on her. And, of course, Valentino, being as smart as he is, asked if we could get some kind of credit, and the producers are getting back to our marketing department to negotiate. So, it turns out, ultimately, to be a good situation for us."

By this time Valentino was looking a lot less disgusted and was smiling and stroking his hair. He looked like a cartoon lion.

"It doesn't erase what you did or the fact that I don't think you can be trusted," Valentino said with both eyebrows raised. "And I've told Craig that I personally don't want to work with someone I can't trust."

I swallowed hard. And even though I didn't especially like Valentino, I had to respect his decision. I stood, ready to leave. At least it didn't look like I was going out in handcuffs. "I understand. I know I made a huge mistake. I'm very sorry for any trouble I've caused you."

Craig Denton stood as well. "Carlos, the trouble you've caused, you've caused for yourself. I've asked Valentino to give you a second chance."

I looked at Valentino. If he'd looked like he was happy to have so much power over what happened to me before, now he looked like he'd won the whole poker game. He leaned forward in my direction, but he wouldn't look at me.

"I'm not one who's big on second chances, especially when it concerns matters of integrity. And I told Craig that I have very mixed feelings about this. But I've decided to"—and this is when he looked up at me—"put you on probation."

I wasn't sure I'd heard him right, but I didn't ask.

"From now until I decide otherwise, I'll be watching you like a hawk. One false move, and you're out."

"I understand. I do. Thank you."

Valentino got up slowly and dramatically. "Oh, don't thank *me*. Not at all. If it weren't for Mr. Denton, you wouldn't have a prayer at FeatureFace, believe me. So I suggest you watch your step."

We all walked to the door and got onto the elevator together. I'd just left my own funeral, and somehow I was still alive.

On the way down I could feel my phone vibrating. I didn't dare take it out.

When we got to the main floor, we walked to the FeatureFace counter. I didn't know exactly what to do, so I blurted out, "Thank you again! I'll see you this weekend."

Craig smiled at me, and Valentino kept walking. It was not going to be easy.

A few feet away from the counter, I took out my phone.

There was a message from Rosalia. So I called her back. I would have put it off because I felt so shook up from the whole FeatureFace thing, but I knew she'd avoided me since Danny had beaten me up and I'd tried to press charges.

"Rosalia? What's up?"

There was a big silence. Then my sister said very quietly, "I'm sorry about what he did to you, Carlos." All I could think of was how many times "I'm sorry" had been said by someone in our family today. I'd said it about fifty times, and now Rosalia, who was definitely not a "sorry" girl at all, was apologizing to me for maybe the first time since we were toddlers.

"It's not so bad," I told her, laughing. "With plastic surgery I'll look almost the same."

"I feel horrible," she said.

"I feel horrible about what he did to *you*. I won't ask you

217

if it's over." But I was hoping she'd tell me what I wanted to hear. When I didn't hear anything, I pretty much had my answer. Who knew what it would take to make her leave Danny? It reminded me of this article we read in psychology about how people who know they have lung cancer keep smoking anyway.

After the silence Rosalia said, "I gotta go, hon."

And I said, "Okay. I guess I'll see you at home." Now all I could do was pray.

I called Shirlena's number. I wanted to leave a message saying thank you for what she'd said to the big boys at FeatureFace. I was surprised when she actually answered.

"Shirlena? This is Carlos."

"Hi, honey. I called your company."

"I know. I wanted to thank you."

"I think it went really well. I'm glad you called. We didn't talk about how you get paid for the show. And we didn't talk about next week. I know you go to school. How is that for you, coming in to do my makeup for the show? I'd love for you to come back, but I don't want to mess around with your school stuff."

"No." That's all I could get out.

"No? So you don't think you can do it?"

"No, I meant it's not interfering with my school stuff. I'm sure I can do it."

"I mean it, Carlos. I'd love to have you, but I don't want to be the cause of you not graduating or something."

"Oh, I promise. You wouldn't be. I mean, there's no problem. Really."

"Okay, then. Let me talk to the producer and let's see how it goes. All right, honey?"

"Yes, Shirlena. Sure."

"You're a talented guy, Carlos."

So I hung up with Shirlena and almost got run over crossing Thirty-fourth Street. I caught a glimpse of myself reflected in a store window. My head was swollen, my face was swollen. I looked like I was on a lunch break from filming a horror movie about tastefully dressed Hispanic high school monsters.

I didn't have a boyfriend—he was something I made up, and yeah, I was still a little embarrassed even though he proved he was a good friend.

And speaking of friends, I'd lost one of my best ones—Soraya-Anna-Wintour. The most I could do was hope with time and payments on the Stella McCartneys, she'd forgive me for being such a big liar.

I'd definitely have to prove myself to Valentino to keep my job.

My sister was crazy about a criminal who had beat me up and left me looking like a piece of dog meat.

But you know what? When I looked at my swollen, scratched-up face looking back at me in the store window reflection, I still saw Carrlos Duarte, makeup artist to the stars! And the rest, sooner or later, I'd figure out.

WHEN ARE YOU TOO FAR IN TO GET OUT?

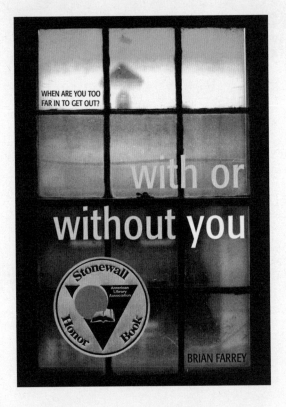

Secrets threaten to destroy friendship and love
in this heartbreaking novel by Brian Farrey.

A STONEWALL HONOR BOOK

LIFE. LOVE. FRIENDSHIP.

From critically acclaimed author Ellen Wittlinger

Love & Lies

Hard Love

Parrotfish

Heart on My Sleeve

Blind Faith

Razzle

Sandpiper

SIMON & SCHUSTER BFYR

TEEN.SimonandSchuster.com

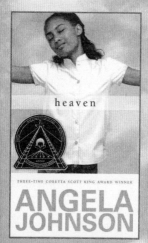